CORDOVA CHRISTMAS

Chanda Stelter

Books by Chanda Stelter

Guitar Ghost Series

Guitar Ghost
Cordova Christmas
A Broken Cord (Coming in the future)
A Cord of Three (Coming in the future)

Acknowledgements

I want to express my deepest gratitude to some very important people whose insight, knowledge, encouragement, and constant support helped bring this story to life.

To my mom, Betty, your years of teaching English sharpened my syntax, flow, and grammar. You also guided me in better capturing the authentic time period of this story. But most of all, thank you for being my lifelong cheerleader. Your unconditional love and steady encouragement have carried me through every chapter of my life. From the little notes you left me on my dresser before a piano recital or after basketball games to your initial reaction after reading the first pages of *Guitar Ghost*: "Chanda Lonae, you wrote this? I think you need to see this through." And now, here I am, publishing the second book in the series. Thank you for believing in me from the very beginning and inspiring me to leap into this journey.

To my sister, Chara, your thoughtful feedback and creative suggestions elevated this book to the next level. You left no stone unturned. Though you apologized for all your scribbles on my draft, I want you to know I cherish every single one. Your comments refined my writing more than you'll ever know. You poured yourself into helping me grow as a writer, and you did it with passion. Thank you for stretching me. I'm endlessly grateful for you.

To my father-in-law, Stan, your sharp editorial eye and experience as an author brought a level of professionalism I couldn't have reached on my own. Your attention to grammar and word usage (or misusage 😊) helped me hone my skills. Thank you for your genuine interest in my writing and belief in me. You emboldened me and made me feel like a real author even when I doubted myself.

To my dear friend, Mary, your generous gift of time and your expertise in formatting, cover templates, and the "order of operations" for publishing were absolutely invaluable. Thank you for walking me through every version and every mistake with such grace, patience, and kindness. I simply couldn't have done this without you.

And finally, to my husband, Shawn, your intellect never ceases to amaze me. You always take things to a deeper level, and our brainstorming sparked some of my favorite little "nuggets" in this story. Thank you for always thinking outside the box and pushing me to do the same. You challenged me to sharpen my sensory awareness and add layers of depth to my writing. And without being too mushy, you are my greatest inspiration for any romance I write.

To Shawn,
My one and only,
my truest inspiration for any love story.
You are my greatest supporter and biggest fan,
the one who keeps me grounded,
and my iron that sharpens iron.

Copyrights

CORDOVA
CHRISTMAS

CONTENTS

Prologue

Saturday, November 12th, 1966

The scent of fried catfish lingered faintly in the living room. Robert sat with his feet kicked up in his well-worn tan recliner, its arms smooth from years of use. With his belly full and an afghan spread across his lap, he felt both content and comfortable as *The Jackie Gleason Show* flickered in black and white on the television screen.

The steady tick of the mantle clock competed with the rhythmic hum of Patty's sewing machine in the dining room, where she was busy mending. Robert glanced over at James and Jessie, curled up on the davenport. They were half-watching the show, half-whispering to each other. Carrie was upstairs taking her bath. Lydia, no doubt, was tucked in her room with her nose buried in a book, same as always.

As the show faded into a commercial break, Robert cleared his throat, more signal than sound. "I've been thinking about it," he said. "Ya can't get married on Saturday, June 4th."

Their heads snapped toward him, Jessie's stomach tightening, heart lurching. "What do you mean?" she asked, her voice uncertain.

"Ya can't get married on Saturday, June 4th," he repeated, his tone unchanged.

A wave of heat swept over her. Her pulse quickened. The walls seemed to inch closer. Her

1

daddy had always been a protective papa bear. But this? It felt out of character, even for him. Why would he backtrack after giving James his blessing? Did he think they were rushing things?

The sewing machine in the next room hummed on, steady and indifferent, but somehow in sync with her spinning thoughts. Jessie took a breath and tried again. "Daddy, I don't understand." Her voice caught. "Why can't we get married?"

"That's not what I mean," Robert replied. "I'm just sayin', ya can't get married on *Saturday*, June 4th."

Jessie blinked, confused. "But…why?"

Robert leaned back, a chuckle escaping. "Because June 4th is a Sunday!"

For a moment, silence filled the room. Then realization. Robert bit back a grin as he watched their expressions shift from confusion to disbelief.

"It's on a Sunday?" James asked, turning to Jessie. "How'd we mess that up?"

Jessie stared at him, then groaned. "I swear the calendar said Saturday." She turned back to her father, hand to her chest. "Landsakes, Daddy! Ya had me as nervous as a long-tailed cat in a room full o' rockin' chairs."

Robert laughed. "When yer mama, who can hardly go a couple days without plannin' somethin', looked at the calendar this mornin', we realized y'all made a little mistake. Figured I better tell ya before Pastor Mark thinks yer tryin' to hijack his Sunday sermons."

Jessie exhaled. "It really is a Sunday? I can't believe we missed that."

"Sure is. So, you've got two options: change the date or start sweet-talkin' Pastor Mark." He gave them a wink. "And between you and me, I'd change the date."

Jessie smiled but then nudged James. "Actually, Daddy, we've been talkin'. When we were picnickin' out at Eden's Pathway this afternoon, we decided we don't wanna wait that long anymore." Her grin widened. "We wanna move the weddin' up...to December 31st. New Year's Eve. And *that*, I *do* know, is a Saturday."

Robert stared at her. "This December? As in seven weeks from now?"

Jessie nodded, her eyes shining with excitement.

"Well, darlin'," Robert said, shaking his head slowly, "then I guess y'all got two people ya need to sweet-talk. Better catch Pastor Mark tomorrow after church, make sure it works with him. And..." He tipped his head toward the dining room. "Ya might wanna call yer mama in here."

He leaned back in his recliner with a laugh. "Lord, have mercy on ya both."

Chapter 1
Preparations

Saturday, December 3rd, 1966

The joyful spirit of Christmas hung in the crisp air. A smile spread across Jessie's face as she busied herself. There was so much to get ready for, but more than the magic of Christmas permeated the air this December. Not only was she busy with all the preparations for Christmas just around the corner, she was also planning a wedding. *Their wedding.* She still couldn't believe that her mother had agreed to moving up the date from June to December so they could marry sooner. As Jessie pictured marrying James, her smile grew wider. It wouldn't just be a day marking their union as man and wife; it would be a celebration of love triumphing over the trials they had endured.

The separation from James while he was in Vietnam had been tough, almost unbearable, but they had proven tougher. It certainly hadn't been easy. Jessie's smile faded as her difficult memories of the past clashed with her joyful anticipation of the future. Their time apart had been more challenging than anything Jessie had ever endured. There were days she didn't think she could keep going, let alone get out of bed. But they had done it. *I have fought the good fight, I have finished the race, I have kept the faith.* Her smile returned. She and James had come

4

out stronger for it, ready to take on the rest of life together as man and wife.

Before James even went to Vietnam, when they first started talking about marriage, he had tossed around the idea of a fall wedding in Eden's Pathway. But with just returning from Vietnam the end of October, Jessie knew there was no way they could pull off planning a wedding that quickly. As it was, her mother nearly had a heart attack when she and James told her they wanted to move it from June to December.

She put her hand to her mouth to stifle her giggle, as if her mother were standing next to her.

What a way to celebrate the New Year's Eve holiday together. And, amidst the Christmas season with all its splendor, the timing would be the perfect backdrop for their wedding. It also felt fitting, since James had given her a promise ring in December two years ago.

Two years ago already. How could that be? Her smile softened and spread, reaching her eyes as the memory surfaced. It had been their senior year, and that Christmas James had given Jessie his mother Rita's wedding ring from his parents' marriage. James's father, Bennett, had passed away from cancer when James was only seven years old, so the ring was very special to him.

Reliving the moment, Jessie sucked in her breath. It had taken her breath away then and now. She would never forget her astonishment upon opening the tiny, worn box. First confusion, then anticipation, and finally awe as she removed the lid to reveal the ornate ring she now wore. Jessie glanced down at her hand. The beautiful ring shimmered back at her.

Jessie's parents had known about the promise ring, because James asked her father Robert's permission to give it to her. Robert never let on, but she knew that this small gesture meant a great deal to her daddy. Jessie let out the breath she didn't realized she was holding. In many ways, that all seemed like a lifetime ago. James had been to Vietnam and back, and she…she had been on her own journey in the process. She had run the race set before them. Shaking her head, she silently prayed. *Thank you, Lord, for keepin' James and me in yer lovin' care.*

Vietnam had given them a new perspective. Live life now. Don't wait on the future as it may not come. Her expression sobered as her thoughts turned to James's good friend, Jim Beau, who had lost his life in battle. Jessie closed her eyes and tilted her head up. Death. The end of life. She took in a deep breath. Jim's short life had harshly reminded James and her to live for the present. She swallowed the lump in her throat. Jessie knew James thought often of Jim. A quote she read earlier that week came to mind by Emily Dickinson: "That it will never come again is what makes life so sweet."

Yes, death, in its finality, had taught them to embrace the present. Hence, their desire not to wait for a June wedding. She had merely traded her summer vision of a reception under the sun in the church courtyard with buckets of his mama's caramels adorning blue gingham-lined tables for a winter reception indoors, where those caramels would sit atop red and green holiday-trimmed tables in the church basement. Jessie hadn't minded the trade at all. In fact, it was the best way she could think to celebrate New Year's Eve.

So now, in just under four weeks, their wedding would take place at First Baptist with Pastor Mark officiating. They were almost finished with their premarital counseling with him. Butterflies of excitement fluttered in Jessie's stomach. Their last session would be this Wednesday. They also planned to meet with his wife, Arlette, who was the church's wedding planner. They'd meet with her just before their session with Pastor Mark. Arlette had been a wonderful help in overseeing the details, and one suggestion from her had been for Jessie to make her own bouquet. Everything seemed to be coming together.

Suddenly, Jessie shook her head, as if awakening from a daze. She looked down at an unfinished bouquet in her hands. Arlette's idea had inspired Jessie to pick up supplies at Fancy's Mercantile on Thursday morning before work. She worked Tuesday and Thursday afternoons at the high school, relieving the school secretary, Mrs. Penderlyn. Jessie had started working there while James was in Vietnam, encouraged by her father to get out of the house and find purpose in her days. At the time, Mrs. Penderlyn was looking to reduce her hours to help her daughter, Clara Sue, with newborn twins. The timing had been serendipitous.

While at Fancy's, Jessie had browsed through catalogs, marveling at the latest trends. Artificial flowers were growing popular. Jessie had chosen a simple teardrop shape for her bouquet and selected three floral stems of red ranunculus so her bouquet, though small, would be dense. She also bought some green floral tape and a few sprigs of Maidenhair fern for some greenery. The fern brought to mind the lush beds in Eden's Pathway where she and James had spent many moments daydreaming of their future together. Although they couldn't marry there as James had once suggested, she could still weave its presence into their wedding.

Jessie glanced at the unfinished bouquet in her lap again. With a quick breath, she resolved to focus. Her mother had plans for her sisters and her to bake Christmas goodies later, and she needed to finish this project. As she picked up the bouquet, her heart swelled. Soon, she would become Mrs. James Theodore Patterson. And, she couldn't wait.

* * *

James pushed open the door as a familiar twinge of pain flared in his shoulder, a sharp reminder of Vietnam. The ache always brought a vivid image with it—Jim Beau's face. Not a day had passed since James last saw his battle buddy that he didn't think of him. Jim had been more than a friend. He was James's backup gunner, his brother in the nightmare of war. Together, they'd saved 31 men in their platoon from a deadly ambush. But in James's eyes, the true hero had always been Jim Beau. Without him, none of those lives would have been spared.

And yet, six were lost. The stab of pain in his shoulder deepened, a physical echo of his grief. Among those lost that fateful day was Jim. The thought haunted him. Precious lives were saved, but precious lives were lost. Jim's death especially served as a constant reminder of how fleeting life is and how priceless.

James's thoughts were interrupted by Linny's voice. The bartender, and owner, of the tavern popped his head up from behind the bar as the sound of the door creaked shut. Squinting, Linny called out, "Jacob, that you?" He was waiting for his daytime help to show up and start mopping.

The smell of stale cigarettes clung stubbornly to the air, the haze of smoke lingering in the dimly lit pub. James inhaled deeply, resisting the familiar urge to light up. The scent, once unnoticed, now seemed to draw him in. He took another deep breath, pausing, letting the air fill his nostrils before he continued walking. His shoes stuck slightly with each step. The red oak hardwood floor, dulled with sticky evidence of last night's revelry, needed Jacob to arrive soon.

"Nope, it's me—James," he called out, moving toward the bar. "James Patterson."

"Well, I'll be darned," Linny said, his tone flat but his eyes betraying a hint of recognition.

"I told y'all I'd be back for another gig," James exclaimed, though his usual enthusiasm evaded him slightly. "Me and the boys are itchin' to get back to ol' times. How 'bout a little holiday hoedown with The Beau Brothers?" He raised his hands theatrically, showcasing the band's name. A faint, wistful smile twitched at one corner of his mouth, the memory of Jim Beau still fresh in his mind. He was touched that Nathaniel, RJ, and Bobby Ray suggested the name in Jim's honor.

When they first met, Jim had shared with James that he was in a family band back in his hometown in Long Prairie, Minnesota, where he played bass guitar. James relentlessly teased him, trying to convince him to move to Cordova and join his band and be his backup because they needed a bass player. The name The Beau Brothers felt like a fitting tribute. Jim's final act as James's "backup" had been lifesaving. For others, not for Jim.

"I could use a little more holiday spirit in here," Linny said, interrupting James's thoughts. "I like the idea."

"Well, that was easy. Ya mean I don't even have to grovel this time?" James teased. His grin wavered as Linny raised an eyebrow. James held up his hands in surrender. "Alright, alright, when would ya like us?"

"How 'bout next Friday night?" Linny suggested. "With the *Light up Cordova* event, there will be lots of people in town. I reckon we could draw quite the crowd this way."

"Ya have yerself a deal," James said, extending his hand.

"Now hold yer horses," Linny replied, not moving. "We haven't settled on the details yet."

James chuckled. Linny always kept his cards close, but that was also one of the things James appreciated most about him. If he made it easy, the win wouldn't be as gratifying. "Alright, Linny. I best hush up and listen to yer terms."

And with that, they hammered out the details for The Beau Brothers' first gig.

* * *

"Lydia Ruth, can ya please start makin' the frostin' for the Sally Ann cookies? They've cooled enough to

10

frost," Patty instructed, while pulling the Christmas bark out of the oven. She inhaled deeply, "Mmm, I can't wait to try this new recipe."

"Me too!" Robert chimed in from his spot at the small table in the corner of the kitchen. A newspaper lay splayed in front of him, but he wasn't really reading it with much interest. He was more focused on soaking in the holiday merriment of his girls as they filled the kitchen with the comforting fragrances of Christmas.

Patty tsked at him, playfully rolling her eyes. Setting the hot pans of bark on a cooling rack, she slipped two more pans into the oven and rotated the dial on her handheld timer. "There," she said, setting the timer on the counter. "Fifteen minutes."

"Mama, where did ya get this Christmas bark recipe?" Carrie asked, her ever-curious nature bubbling to the surface.

"Ida Mae," Patty replied. "She says it's the latest recipe for the season or so Ida Mae claims. But leave it to her to always know what's new." Patty shook her head, her lips pursed in a smug expression. "Carrie Grace, I'd like ya to wash the Spam tin and dry it right away so it doesn't rust. Then stick it in the pantry so it's ready for the next time we wanna cut out the Sally Anns. Thank ya, dear."

"Yes, Ma'am," Carrie said with a nod and an exaggerated salute. "I'll make sure it's spick and span, or rather..." she paused, a goofy grin tugging at her lips. "Spick and Spam." She giggled at her own joke.

Lydia shook her head, "Always, Carrie Grace. Always."

"Always what?" Carrie chirped.

"Oh, nothin'," Lydia replied, smiling. "Ya just always know how to add a little *extra* to the moment."

"And we love ya all the more for it," Patty added warmly. Then she turned to Jessie May. "Now, if we're still plannin' on makin' Lydia's favorite iced sugar cookies and yer daddy's old-fashioned thumb print cookies—"

"That's why I'm here!" Robert cut in.

"Hush now, Mr. Sit-there-in-the-corner-doin'-nothin', or ya can get on over here and make yerself useful." Robert, quick to obey Patty's teasing rebuke, flicked his paper up to eye level. He busied himself with the act of reading. "That's what I thought, Mister!" Patty said, shaking her head. The girls burst into giggles, which earned them a playfully stern glance from their mother. "See what you've started, Mr. Clark?"

"I don't know what yer talkin' about," Robert replied, feigning innocence. He cast a conspiratorial glance toward the girls, who tried to stifle their laughter.

Rolling her eyes, Patty smiled and continued, "Jessie May, we're gonna need more eggs. Lydia Ruth picked earlier this mornin', but those Johnny-come-lately hens are always good for a few more. I heard them a cacklin', so I'm guessin' there's more eggs. Can ya go check and do the second pickin'?"

"I can do that, but make sure yer watchin' the timer. We don't wanna burn the last batch of bark."

"Heavens, I'm glad ya reminded me," Patty huffed. "That old timer tends to get stuck the last bit more often than not and doesn't ding at me." She tilted her head towards Robert. "I need a new timer for Christmas." She coyly batted her eyes at Robert who was "reading" his newspaper, but she knew better. He was listening. She sighed. "Land sakes, Jessie May, what am I goin' to do when ya get married and leave me?"

"Mama, do ya think that once I'm married, I won't come bake cookies with y'all anymore?"

"Well," Patty said, her voice cracking with emotion. "A mama's not sure her place anymore once her children leave the nest." Tears began to pool in her eyes, betraying the spirited mood of the day.

"Oh, Mama, come here." Jessie May embraced her mother in a tender hug.

Patty sniffled, hastily collecting her composure. "Now, shoo! Go on and get those eggs, girl. Yer gettin' me all choked up again." Patty waved her off with a forced smile.

"Okay, okay!" Jessie May laughed, pulling off her apron and tossing it on the counter. She grabbed the round metal basket that sat on the floor by the back door. As she opened the door, a waft of cool air pushed into the room. She tossed her head back and called out, "Back in a jiffy!"

Patty sucked in a quick breath, stifling the unwanted tears that threatened to spill over. Glancing at the sink, she spotted Carrie playing in the suds. "Goodness gracious, child. Yer slower than molasses washin' that tin. Finish up, darlin', or we'll be here 'til the cows come home."

"But Mama, we don't have cows. We have chickens," Carrie corrected with a mischievous grin.

Lydia shook her head. "Just finish washin', Carrie Grace."

The last of the Christmas goodies had cooled and were already stacked on shelves in the coolness of their entryway. Patty was wiping the kitchen countertop with slow, deliberate strokes when Robert broke the silence.

"Now that yer done with the bakin', come on over here, woman, and give me some sugar."

Patty turned and shot him a look, her hands resting on her hips, mouth pursed like she'd just tasted something sour.

"Okay," Robert tried again, "come on over here, *please*, Mrs. Clark, and give me some sugar."

"That's better," she said, sauntering over to him. She stooped to give him a kiss, and Robert scooted his chair back from the table, patting his lap.

Patty sat down with a sigh. "I am plumb worn slap out. These girls this year have me busier than a moth in a mitten." She blew a strand of hair from her face with an exaggerated puff of air.

"This year?" Robert raised an eyebrow.

"Yes, I don't know what's different?"

"Could it maybe, possibly, be that it's not just Christmas preparations but also plannin' a weddin' that has ya all tuckered out? Or maybe…" Robert's slow southern drawl stretched out the last words.

"Or maybe what?" Patty asked, falling for his bait.

"Maybe yer gettin' older?"

"Robert Christopher Clark!" Patty huffed, glaring at him. Then with a slow gentle motion, she brought her body against his. Leaning in close to his ear with a sultry tone meant only for him, she whispered, "That's not what ya told me last night."

Robert's breath hitched. "Pats, careful what ya start cookin' in this kitchen ya know ya can't finish." His voice was thick and breathy. Unheeding his warning, she batted her lashes. Before he could say anymore, the doorbell chimed. "Saved by the bell, ya little temptress," he chuckled, patting his wife's thigh as a cue to stand. He folded his newspaper and tossed it onto the ever-growing stack beside him. "I'll get it," he said, pushing to his feet. But as he reached the swinging door, he turned and gave her a slight shake of his head, wagging his finger. "Yer gonna be the death of me, woman." And with that, he disappeared through the door.

* * *

Still shaking his head, Robert opened the front door to find a familiar face. It had been a month and a half since James had returned and every time he saw him, Robert was filled with thankfulness. "Well, good afternoon, James. Come on in. The girls just finished their Christmas bakin'."

"I can smell it. Smells amazin' in here." Lowering his voice, he covertly leaned in towards Robert and put his hand up to the side of his mouth. "Are they allowin' any samplin'?"

Robert chuckled. "I think that can be arranged. But first, let's go have us a sit in the livin' room for a minute. There's somethin' I've been meanin' to visit with ya about." He swung his arm out in a gesture toward the living room, inviting James in. Then he turned and walked to the bottom of the staircase and hollered up the stairs. "Jessie Maaaay! James is here!"

Robert hadn't even had a chance to get comfortable in his recliner when he heard the thunderous sound of Jessie's feet barreling down the stairs. She burst into the room, out of breath and all smiles.

"James!" She plopped down beside James on the davenport, barely leaving any space between them.

"You two are like white on rice," Robert teased.

"Daddy, I waited a long time to be near James, so ya better just get used to this," she blurted.

Robert attempted a stern expression, but a smile quickly broke through. "Well, I can't argue with that," he said, casting a fond glance at his daughter. Her joy was contagious. Jessie returned his smile. It felt so good to see her smiling, so full of happiness. Robert couldn't help but feel excited for Jessie and James's future together. That thought redirected his focus to what he wanted to visit about. "James, I have a proposition for ya."

"Now ya have me curious, Robert," James said with a questioning tone.

Robert lowered his footrest of his recliner and sat up straighter. "I know you've put college on hold since comin' back, and I understand that." He glanced at his daughter. Jessie's smile widened and she grabbed James' hand. Robert continued. "I have been talkin' with Chuck, and he's thinkin' about phasin' out of the shop…he's been strugglin' more with his MS. He's asked me to take over all of the managin', but then I'll need someone to help take over some of my service work. There is a lot to do and little time to do it. It's hard work for fair wages. I would help to train you. So, what do ya think?"

James took a deep breath, digesting the offer. What his words suggested went beyond offering a mere job. This was more than a job offer. It was the act of taking care of him. The extending of a father's love and provision. Since James was seven years old, he hadn't had a father figure to look out for him as Robert was doing. His mother Rita had married John, his step-daddy, about five years ago now. And though that relationship was good, they never strained it by having John try to be a father figure when he came into James's life at 15 years old. His relationship with John was more of an amicable friendship and he was content with that.

But as he sat staring across the room at Jessie's father, who was patiently waiting for an answer, James was so grateful. Marrying Jessie meant he was gaining a father again. He could see the concern in Robert's eyes. Robert shifted slightly in his chair as the silence held the room in a climax. Just then James realized that both Robert and Jessie were staring at him waiting and wondering.

"Robert, I would be honored to accept the job. Thank you for thinkin' of me." James squeezed Jessie's hand as he spoke, emotion tightening his voice.

Robert's face lit up. "I'm glad to hear that, son. For a moment there, with ya hesitatin', I thought ya maybe were goin' to say no."

"It wasn't hesitation, Robert. It was gratitude," James replied, his voice faltering as emotion overcame him.

Robert rose to his feet and walked over to James and Jessie, pulling them into a warm embrace. In that quiet moment, no more words were needed. Everything that mattered was conveyed in the strength of his arms and the steadfast presence of a father's unconditional love.

* * *

Wednesday, December 7th, 1966

Pastor Mark leaned back in his chair, one leg casually crossed over the other. The slow, rhythmic creak of the chair accompanied his easy rocking motion. His voice, calm yet firm, filled the space. "As we wrap up yer marriage counselin' tonight, there's somethin' y'all need to know." He paused, captivating their attention. "Y'all are ready."

Seated across from his desk, James and Jessie exchanged pleased smiles. Jessie's grew into a doe-eyed grin directed at James, who took her hand and gave it a reassuring squeeze. A soft clearing of Pastor Mark's throat brought their attention back. Uncrossing his leg, he leaned forward, resting both feet firmly on the floor. His elbows settled on the desk as his fingers came together in a steeple. He tapped his fingertips lightly together, punctuating his words as he spoke, "But, there's nothin' I can say greater than this…"

His words hung in the air, the steady ticking of the clock on the paneled wall amplifying the silence. James and Jessie shifted in their chairs, the weight of his pause commanding their full attention. "There's no more *just* James and Jessie." Both furrowed their brows. He paused again, his voice measured. "A marriage takes three." He tapped the words out with a pulsed succession of his fingertips, then let silence linger a bit longer. "Y'all know what I mean by that?"

Jessie answered softly, "Yes, Sir. We need the Lord in our marriage."

Pastor Mark nodded. "Yes, and not just *in* yer marriage but *over* it. He must be Lord over every part of yer life together. Everythin', from this day forward, begins and ends with Him. If ya want yer marriage to last a lifetime, it must have the *essence of eternity*...God."

James and Jessie nodded in unison.

"So, always remember that a marriage takes three. Never forget it." Pastor Mark extended his hands across the desk. "Let us close in prayer."

James and Jessie leaned forward, clasping Pastor Mark's hands. Bowing their heads, the three formed a small circle of prayer.

"Dear Heavenly Father," Pastor Mark began, "we thank thee for this time over the past six weeks, preparin' James and Jessie May for holy matrimony. As we come before ya now, Lord, in a circle of three, let these two young people be bound to you as a cord of three. May they never stray from yer presence, dear Lord. Bless them and fill them with yer Holy Spirit. Guide them. Lead them. And yes, Lord, even convict them. For we know from yer word that love keeps no record of wrongs. Grant them yer grace to overlook flaws and root them in yer love as ya prepare their hearts to join as one. We ask all this in yer holy name. Amen."

Lifting their heads, Pastor Mark released their hands and smiled. "Congratulations to ya both."

He stood and walked them to the door. "Well, I'll see y'all at yer final session."

James tilted his head, a quizzical look on his face. "Wasn't this our last session, Pastor Mark?"

"No," Pastor Mark replied with a sly glint in his eyes. "Yer ceremony is the final session. There's a yes-or-no pop quiz at the end…James, do you take Jessie May Clark to be yer lawfully wedded wife for better or worse?"

James rubbed his chin theatrically. "Hmm, I might need to think about the *worse* part."

"James Theodore Patterson!" Jessie gasped, her voice rising to a higher pitch.

Laughing, Pastor Mark raised his hands, volunteering a surrender. "All right, all right. I reckon I set that reaction in motion." He turned to Jessie with a twinkle in his eye. "Before ya get madder than a wet hen, I'll call it a day."

His laughter followed them out as the office door closed behind them.

Chapter 2
Light up Cordova

Friday, December 9th, 1966

"Carrie Grace," Patty called up the stairs, cupping her hands around her mouth, "make sure ya put a sweater on!"

She turned to Robert, who sat tying his boots on the entryway bench. "It's goin' to be cold as a frosted frog tonight, especially with that breeze and moisture hangin' in the air." She gave an involuntary shiver and rubbed her arms. "Can ya grab the scarves I left on the kitchen table? I want to pack those in my bag. It'll be downright chilly by the end of the night, especially if Carrie wants to see Santa's big appearance after the parade. And Clarence Jackson is doin' his wagon rides again, so we'll all be wantin' those scarves."

"Yes, dear," Robert replied, giving a good-natured nod as he started toward the kitchen. Then he paused mid-step and glanced back over his shoulder. "Ya want to check if Jessie May and Lydia Ruth are ready?"

"Oh, heavens, that's right!" Patty smacked her forehead lightly. "You don't even know there's been a change of plans. Jessie isn't here."

Robert furrowed his brow in confusion. "What do ya mean, she's not here?"

21

"While you were sawin' logs in yer chair, she left to go meet up with Betty Lou and Karren Norraine." Patty explained, brushing her hair from her face. "They wanted to head in early, see if they could catch The Beau Brothers warmin' up, since they aren't allowed inside Linny's for the gig."

"Well, I'll be! I must've been plumb out cold. I didn't hear a blessed thing."

"Oh, ya stacked quite a log pile with all that snorin'," Patty teased, and Robert answered with a cheeky grin and light pat on her backside. "Say now," she scolded playfully, shooing him away with a laugh. "Anyway, we'll meet Jessie May in town. And yes, Lydia Ruth is ready. She's holed up in her room readin', naturally. Said to holler when we're ready to leave."

"Alright, I'll grab the scarves and check on Carrie Grace. We both know *that one*," he tilted his head toward the stairway, "is more likely settin' up a teddy bear tea party instead of gettin' ready."

Patty chuckled, shaking her head with fond exasperation. "Well, don't let her dawdle. We best get to leavin' if we want to browse the booths before the parade starts."

"I'll pop into Lydia's room and get her movin'." He stepped toward the kitchen, then paused, his eyes softening as they met hers. There was a tenderness in his gaze that made her chest tighten. A look she knew was hers alone. He smiled, his voice warm with affection. "Cordova Christmas, here we come."

* * *

Karen Norraine, Betty Lou and Jessie May agreed to meet by the big Christmas tree downtown near Town Square. When they arrived, a group of carolers from the First Baptist choir were singing "O Come, All Ye Faithful," filling the evening with rich harmonious sounds of Christmas. Pastor Mark and his wife, Arlette, stood nearby, handing out steaming cups of mulled cider.

The three young women spotted each other at the same time and waved enthusiastically as they hustled toward one another. When they came together, they embraced in a jubilant group hug, laughing with unrestrained joy. Their greeting was fueled by their youthful energy.

"I've been so excited for tonight!" Karen Norraine's voice broke the moment and the group hug dissolved.

"Me too," Jessie May replied, her tone brimming with excitement. She held onto an inner thought that this would be her last Cordova Christmas spent single and carefree with her friends. "Let's grab some hot cider from Pastor Mark and Arlette. I'm already gettin' chilled."

"Good idea, but we need to keep an eye on the time. My mama wants me to meet up with them for a wagon ride and sit together for the parade," Betty Lou added.

"Same," said Jessie, "but we have lots of time. Let's get some cider and then see if we can slip into Linny's to hear the guys warmin' up. If they've started playin' already, maybe we can just stand in the doorway and listen."

"There's no way we're gettin' in. Y'all realize that, right?" Karen Norraine stated.

"I know, I just figured standin' by the doorway won't hurt nobody."

"We'll see," Karen said skeptically. "Ol' Linny will still be on us like flies on honey if we're blockin' traffic."

"I think, with all the festivities, he'll be less strict. I really want to hear them play. Are ya gals willin' to try?" Jessie asked.

"Of course! We wanna hear The Beau Brothers' first gig too," Betty Lou exclaimed, rubbing her hands together to keep warm. "Now, about that cider!"

* * *

Main Street was bustling by the time Robert and Patty drove into town, its charm magnified by the holiday glow. Strings of multicolored lights crisscrossed the street above, casting a whimsical hue over the scene. Light poles were merrily adorned with colorful, fragrant wreaths, filling the crisp air with the unmistakable scent of pine. Local businesses flaunted their festive flair, each storefront an invitation of twinkling displays and booths set up on the sidewalks. Merchants vied for attention, offering a variety of merchandise, holiday sales, and tantalizing seasonal treats.

Robert eased their Plymouth Fury into a narrow spot behind Buckie's BBQ, a location he considered perfect. It was tucked in the alley but centrally located on Main Street, just steps from the heart of the festivities. As the car doors creaked open, Patty reminded the girls to stay close and stick together. Before they stepped into the busy crowd, Robert reached for Patty's hand, gently stilling her. A quiet reminder. A shared breath. His look said it all. *Slow down, take this in, don't let worry steal the moment.*

She paused and inhaled deeply. The scent of barbeque mingled with woodsmoke and the winter air. Nodding with a soft smile, she squeezed his hand. His big hand was warm, hers already chilly. Even though the temperature barely nudged over 40 degrees, an inviting warmth radiated throughout the crowd amidst the shared camaraderie of neighbors. The *Light up Cordova* event wasn't just an annual gathering; it was a cherished tradition.

Together, they walked hand in hand, weaving down the dim alley toward the glowing bustle of Main Street. The crowd thickened as they emerged. The hum of laughter, cheerful greetings, and carolers' melodies enveloped them. Families strolled arm in arm, and children's faces were full of wonder.

"Wow!" Carrie Grace gasped, her own eyes wide with awe as the first burst of the lights came into view. "I see Fancy!" she announced. "Can we go over to her booth?"

"Her name isn't Fancy. It's Fanny," Lydia corrected.

"Well, then why is her store called Fancy's Mercantile?" Carrie asked.

"Actually, her name is Frances," Patty lovingly interrupted. She knew all too well her middle daughter's short tolerance with her younger daughter's incessant questions.

"Frances?" Carrie's voice was high-pitched, carrying the nasaled sound of her Southern drawl. "Then why in tarnation is her store called Fancy's Mercantile?"

"Her name is Frances, but she's gone by Fanny for as long as I can remember. It was her husband Frank who started callin' her Fancy. I believe when they were courtin'."

"That's confusin'. Maybe we should call her Fancy Fanny?"

"That sounds ridiculous, Carrie Grace. You wear me slap out." Lydia's tone held obvious annoyance.

"Girls, that's enough," Robert joined in. He had remained silent up to this point, privately entertained by the conversation of his girls.

"I didn't do nothin'," Carrie huffed, crossing her arms across her chest in stubborn protest. "She's the one who looks like someone licked the red off her candy," Carrie pouted, not liking the gentle reprimand from her father. Then pausing, a comical look suddenly appearing, she said, "Maybe someone licked the red off her Christmas candy cane."

"Oh, my daughter!" Patty shook her head and gave a quick side hug to Carrie. "Yes, let's shoot over to Fanny's. I always love that she decorates with the nativity. Which reminds me, I'd like to look at her nativity sets. I don't have one and I've been wantin' one."

They crossed the street and casually strolled up to Fancy's Mercantile booth. Fanny saw them coming and waved, shouting, "Merry Cordova Christmas, Clarks! Y'all help yerselves to some roasted chestnuts and hot apple cider. And while y'all are enjoyin' a treat, please take a look around." She turned to Robert exuberantly. "Is yer holiday shoppin' done for Patty? I might have just the thing to tickle her fancy."

"Ya want to be tickled?" Carrie asked with a mischievous look in her eyes. Everyone couldn't help but break into laughter, even Lydia.

"Why don't ya ladies admire Fanny's tables while I get us some apple cider," Robert smiled and then pausing, he looked directly at Carrie, "But, don't touch!"

As he was pouring the apple cider and dishing up roasted chestnuts for his girls, he discreetly caught Fanny. Leaning in, he spoke to her in a quiet voice. "I noticed yesterday when I passed by that ya had a lighted stable set up with a colorful nativity display, but I don't see that out today."

"Oh yes, right over there on that table." Fanny let her eyes dart to the table behind her so she wouldn't draw Patty's attention. "I've got a couple stable options. There's a simple unlit one for three dollars, or for only two dollars more, ya can get one that lights up." She cupped her hand near her mouth and leaned closer to whisper. "Personally, I'd go with the plug-in model." She cast a quick glance toward Patty, making sure she was still busy looking with the girls. Then, turning back to Robert, she added in a hushed tone, "As for nativity sets, I've got two styles. One is a beautifully hand-painted ceramic and goes for about $14. The other's a more affordable option made of celluloid. That's a durable kind of plastic, and still real pretty. I'd go with that one. It's practical *and* on sale for five bucks."

"Sold! I'll take the light-up stable and the plastic nativity set," he said, pausing. "But not now." Dropping his voice even lower, he leaned in. "How about Monday? Midmornin' I could swing by before I head to Chuck's. That work for ya?"

"I'll have it all wrapped and ready." She gave a quick nod, and noticing Patty was coming their way, she changed the subject. "I can 'bout imagine y'all are gettin' real excited for yer weddin' bells. Are y'all ready for Jessie May's big day?"

"I don't know if a daddy is ever ready to give away his daughter," Robert answered.

"Y'all aren't givin' away a daughter. Yer gainin' a son." Fanny was never shy to give her opinion and, this time, Robert was grateful. He smiled and nodded his head.

Robert turned and handed the cider to Lydia and Patty. "Here y'all go." Then he handed a cup to Carrie that was less full, adding, "Be careful, Carrie Grace, this is hot." He rubbed his chin as if contemplating. "Well, I reckon it's time to be movin' on. We have Santa to catch up to." He winked at Carrie.

"Thank you, Fanny, for the goodies," Patty said, giving a warm, appreciative smile.

"Y'all are welcome! And, Merry Christmas! I'll see ya at the weddin'!" She turned so only Robert could see her face and raised her eyebrows. *See ya Monday* were the unspoken words translated between the two.

Robert, Patty, Lydia and Carrie gave Fanny a friendly wave and continued up the festive street. Next door, twinkling lights framed the windows of Bromberg's Fine Jewelry, their display tables modest in comparison to the storefront's elegant glow.

"Oh look, they have hot cocoa and gingerbread cookies!" Carrie squealed, bouncing slightly on her toes. "But I declare, I don't see much to look at on their tables."

"They keep most of the jewelry inside," Lydia replied knowingly. "Too expensive to leave out. The treats are just the bait. Once they've lured ya in with the gingerbread cookies and cocoa, they expect you to head inside."

"Well, I'm hooked," Carrie admitted, already drifting toward the tables, her nose twitching at the warm, spicy scent of gingerbread.

"Hold yer horses! This place is too rich for my taste," Patty chimed in. "We've already got treats, and fancy jewels is not what I want or need for Christmas."

"Speak for yerself, Mama. Maybe *I* want some fine jewels. Ya know, even baby Jesus got gold for Christmas," Carrie quipped.

Robert and Patty exchanged amused looks. "We'll keep that in mind," Robert acknowledged. "So, I take it ya changed yer mind about the Midge doll and Spirograph?"

"Oh no, Daddy, I still want those too," Carrie replied without hesitation.

"Well now," Robert said, raising an eyebrow, "ya might have to reconsider that if jewels are being added to yer list. Jewelry is expensive," Robert countered.

Carrie scrunched her eyebrows, clearly weighing the options. "Ya know, on second thought, I think I'll just stop for the cookie."

Patty stifled her laughter. "That's a wise choice, but I think yer hands are already full."

"But I'd rather the gingerbread cookie than the chestnuts."

"Ah, Pats, if she's willin' to give up the jewels, she's earned a gingerbread cookie, don't ya think?" He nodded to Carrie. "Go ahead, darlin'. But, use yer manners and make it quick 'cause I heard Santa and Mrs. Claus are waitin' next to the community tree."

Without another word, Carrie hustled over to Bromberg's booth. Making sure to say her thanks as instructed, she beamed while accepting a cookie. Rejoining her family, she carefully balanced her cider in one hand and the gingerbread cookie in her other as a grin came over her face. "Daddy, do ya think Santa would trade me gold for this cookie and chestnuts? I'll give him two for one."

Robert chuckled, shaking his head as they strolled toward the square. "Darlin', I don't think Santa keeps much gold in his pockets to trade. He's more into milk and cookies than jewels."

Carrie's eyes twinkled. "Well, if he does, I'm willin' to negotiate."

Patty laughed softly, slipping her arm through Robert's. "Oh, Robert, this youngest child of ours just might end up costing us the most."

Completely unfazed, Carrie took a theatrical bite of her cookie. "Worth every penny," she said through a mouthful of crumbs.

The family once again busted into laughter, their hearts light as they continued toward the town square, savoring the simple joy of being together.

* * *

Jessie and the gals managed to catch James, RJ, Bobby Ray, and Nathaniel warming up and even got to hear their first couple of songs. They opened with a piece James had written himself, titled "When I Knew." To most, it sounded like a heartfelt love ballad, but Jessie knew better. She understood its deeper meaning. She knew it was about the moment James's mother, Rita, had emerged from her grief.

After James's father Bennett passed away, Rita had been consumed by sorrow. Her heart shattered from losing the love of her life. Jessie remembered James sharing the intimate details of those darks days his family had endured. For weeks, Rita did little more than shuffle from her bed to the living room chair. Her color had grown pale, her spirit even more so. Each day bled into the next without even the faintest smile or shift in mood.

During that season of heaviness, James's sister Elizabeth became the caretaker of both her mother and little brother. She hadn't had a choice. She simply did what needed to be done. She woke James for school, made sure he was fed, even if it was just a bowl of cereal or a Spam sandwich, did the laundry and took on the responsibility of paying the bills.

They had weathered a great deal during those long weeks after his father died, and while the whole family bore the weight, it was Elizabeth who had caried the heaviest burden. James had been so young then, too little to remember much. However, one moment had stayed with him, a day Pastor Mark came to check on his mama and something shifted.

James had told Jessie how Pastor Mark, as always, brought his Bible and read a passage to offer solace. With the verse Pastor Mark read that day, something stirred his mama, something greater than her grief, pulling her out of the darkness and into the light. The verse he read awakened something deep within her, changing the course of her life…their lives.

Jessie had memorized that verse. *1 John 4:4, "He who is in you is greater than he who is in the world."*

That was the moment Rita always spoke of, the moment she knew. She knew that the God of the universe, whose very essence is love, would carry her out of the valley of the shadow of death. Rita realized she could move forward, even without Bennett. And from that point on, she believed that same source of love would one day help her to find love again.

Jessie felt goosebumps rise along her arms just thinking about it. "When I Knew" held such profound meaning for James. It encapsulated a pivotal moment in his family's story, a testimony of resilience and faith. And as she watched the crowd respond to the song, a wave of pride surged through her. Her heart swelled with gratitude to witness such a special *first* for The Beau Brothers.

Linny's Tavern grew livelier and more crowded by the minute as more patrons filled the space. The girls exchanged a glance, one that said it was time to leave. As they slipped out, Jessie silently hoped James had spotted her in the crowd. Their chatter echoed along Main Street, where the glow of storefronts cast elongated shadows as they made their way back toward their families and the parade. Before parting ways, they agreed to meet again later. The night was young, after all. And so were they.

* * *

A rush of adrenaline shot through James when he scanned the crowd while playing their first song. It

32

was exhilarating. Their band was finally playing a gig and he was singing a song he wrote no less. James could hardly take it all in. As his eyes danced across the crowd, James suddenly noticed one person. That one person almost took his breath away and held his attention the remainder of the night.

Hank Timball was staggering as he walked across the tavern to the front and grabbed a barstool. He was drunk already, nearly missing his stool when he sat down. James watched as Hank ordered another drink he clearly didn't need and then found a table by himself toward the back of the room.

As hard as he tried, he couldn't take his eyes from that area the rest of the night while they played. He hadn't seen Hank since before Vietnam. The room swayed a bit as he sucked in a quick breath. Faltering for a brief moment while singing, Nathaniel shot James a questioning look. James knew he better focus on their music. He'd catch Hank after playing.

* * *

The Beau Brothers played two encore songs. James, RJ, Bobby Ray, and Nathaniel soaked in the rush of it all, elated by the reception they'd received. Linny caught James immediately afterward. Though he wasn't one to dish out compliments, James knew their band had earned the ultimate praise when Linny handed over the payment and said, "When can y'all play again, kid?"

The guys were buzzing with excitement, anxious to meet up with the girls and share the thrill of the night. RJ couldn't wait to see his girlfriend, Landa, while Bobby Ray was eager to find Janet. Of

33

course, their plans also included meeting Jessie May, Karen Norraine, and Betty Lou.

"Y'all go on ahead. I'll catch up in a little bit," James nudged.

"No way," Bobby Ray protested, shaking his head. "Last time ya said that, ya done went and signed up for the Army. So, come on, Jimbo."

James cringed. He really needed to tell them to stop calling him that. It hurt too much. But not tonight. "Go on ahead. I'll be along shortly. I need to find someone."

"Who? Don'tcha need to track down Jessie May. Um, yer future wife?" Nathaniel teased, as if James needed a reminder.

Cutting to the chase, James shot back, "I see Hank over there. Hank Timball."

At the mention of Hank's name, understanding dawned on Nathaniel, RJ, and Bobby Ray.

"I'm sorry, James," Nathaniel murmured. "We should've known."

"It's okay. How were y'all to know?"

"Well, I noticed him walk…er, I mean, stumble in while we were playin'. I should've thought about how that might affect ya. I'm really sorry, James," Nathaniel apologized, his voice barely a whisper. "Go ahead, I'll find Jessie May and let her know you'll be along soon."

* * *

James walked over to Hank's table. "Mind if I join ya?" he asked, gesturing to the empty chair. Hank nodded, and James sat down.

Hank took a sip of his bourbon. "Ya want one?" He pointed to his glass. "It helps, ya know."

James knew what he meant before Hank continued. "It takes the edge off the memories…and the pain when people on the street give ya the middle finger." Hank took another sip of his bourbon, hissing as the amber liquid burned its way down his throat. "Ya don't feel isolated when ya don't feel anythin'." He tilted his head back, draining his tumbler, and set the empty glass on the table a little harder than necessary. "So, do ya want one?"

"I'm not 21 yet," James replied.

Hank waved it off. "Doesn't matter."

"With Linny, it sure does."

"Not if ya just stay here, and I order it. They already carded me. Hells bells, act like yer 21. Ya just finished a blasted gig, and you're thirsty. They won't say a thing."

James hesitated but nodded, feeling a little anxious as he watched Hank stagger toward the bar.

* * *

Jessie spotted James walking along the opposite side of Main Street. She lifted her hand and started waving as soon as she saw him. "There's James!" she called out to the rest of the group.

Nathaniel nudged her shoulder. "See? Told ya he'd catch up. Nothin' to worry about."

As James approached, Nathaniel studied him closely, silently hoping for his own reassurance. He searched James's face for any sign that something was amiss. For a fleeting second, a shadow flickered behind James's eyes, but then his features brightened with his warm, familiar smile, the playful sparkle

35

once again reflecting in his eyes. Nathaniel exhaled, reassured.

"Y'all ready to have some fun?" James whooped, his voice rising above the noise of the crowd. The group responded with a chorus of excited hollers.

Leaning in, James gave Jessie a quick kiss. He felt at ease, just like Hank said he would. The bourbon had helped. It did wonders for chasing away the bite of the cold…and settling something deeper inside him.

* * *

Jessie thought she smelled alcohol on James's breath when he kissed her. But how could that be? He didn't drink, and where would he have gotten it? Nathaniel told her that James would be late since he was settling up with Linny and finagling their next gig. Besides, Linny wouldn't serve James alcohol. He wasn't 21 yet.

And…was that cigarette smoke she tasted with his kiss?

Jessie glanced at James. He looked normal, relaxed. She shook off her worry and breathed a sigh of relief. There was nothing to be concerned about.

Chapter 3
A Happy *New* Year

Monday, December 12th, 1966

Monday, December 12th, 1966

The smell of eggs and bacon was inviting as Robert swung through the door of the kitchen. "Mmm, smells good, Pats," he said, settling into his usual spot at the small table by the window. Robert liked the way the morning light poured in, making it the perfect place to read his paper.

Patty set a bowl in front of him, along with a dish of butter. "Ya want yer bacon and eggs now or after yer grits?"

"I'll take it all at once this mornin', please. I'm in a bit of a hurry," Robert replied.

Patty raised an eyebrow but said nothing. She hustled over to the stove, mindful not to let Robert's eggs overcook. He preferred them runny. Turning off the front burner for the frying pan with his bacon and eggs, she grabbed the kettle from the back burner and took it over to Robert. She ladled a portion of the grits into his bowl and returned the kettle to its place to keep warm. Then, she dished two eggs and two strips of bacon from the pan onto a plate she'd set aside on the counter.

She brought the plate to the table and set it in front of him. "Yer eggs and bacon, my love." She batted her eyes at him with a cheerful smile.

Robert smiled back, his heart full of gratitude for his wife. "Thank ya, sweetheart. Very appreciated."

Patty returned to the sink, where the breakfast dishes from Lydia Ruth and Carrie Grace were stacked, waiting to be washed. With the girls already off to school, it was time to get started on the cleaning.

Robert bowed his head to say grace for his food. After a moment of giving thanks, he picked up the Monday edition of the *Walker County Tribune* Patty had thoughtfully set on top of his pile. Unfolding the paper, Robert scanned the headlines. One quickly caught his eye: "U.S. Bombers Hit Key Hanoi Targets Amid Escalating Vietnam Conflict." A deep sigh escaped his lips. He was so thankful James was back home. His injury had guaranteed he wouldn't be sent back for another tour, but Robert's heart ached for all the young men and women still over there.

Robert set the paper on the table and closed his eyes to pray. *Heavenly Father, thank you for bringin' James home safely. My heart overflows with gratitude, but it also aches for the countless fathers and mothers who haven't been as blessed. Lord, I lift up the young men and women still in Vietnam, facin' dangers I can hardly imagine. Protect them, Father, shield them from harm, and bring comfort to their families who wait with anxious hearts. Bring those young men and women home safely, dear Lord. For this I humbly ask and pray. Amen.*

Opening his eyes, Robert picked up the paper again, smoothing it taunt. His gaze fell on another headline: "NASA Advances Lunar Program with

Apollo Preparations Underway." Robert shook his head and called over his shoulder, "Patty, can ya imagine someone really walkin' on the moon? It's goin' to happen. Ya wait and see."

Patty, elbow-deep in soapy water, didn't answer. Too busy scrubbing the frying pan, she hadn't heard him.

Robert shrugged and kept reading. "Surf-Rock Sensation Sweeps Nation, Beach Boys' 'Good Vibrations' Tops Charts." He skimmed past that article, uninterested, until his eyes landed on another headline: "Civil Rights Movement Gains Momentum as Calls for Equality Rise."

Perusing through the details of the article, he read about the Southern Christian Leadership Conference, marches, and the motivations of young students everywhere who were driving change. Robert felt hopeful about the progress being made but knew there was still much work to be done.

"Can ya lift the paper so I can give the table a wipin'?" Patty asked, standing over him with a dishrag in one hand, her other hand on her hip.

"Yes, Ma'am. I'm just about done." Robert tapped his index finger on another headline. "Look at this: New York Braces for Winter Blizzard, State of Emergency Declared." He shook his head. "It may be 36 degrees here, but we'll hit almost 55 by this afternoon. No snow for us." He picked up the paper so Patty could wipe the table.

"Well, it's still cold enough for the chickens to be wearin' socks," Patty stated, giving a grin as she wiped his spot.

Robert chuckled. "True enough. Which reminds me, I best get the car started so it has a chance to warm up a bit." Folding the paper, he tossed it onto his ever-growing pile, a source of contention with his wife.

"Why ya startin' the car so early? It's only 8:30."

"I told Chuck I'd come in early today. We need to iron out the details for James. Chuck wants him to start after the first of the year when he and Jess get back from their honeymoon."

Satisfied with his answer, Patty nodded, missing the little smirk on Robert's face as he stood.

"Thanks for breakfast, darlin'. It was delicious as usual. And thanks for the sugar." He leaned in and stole a kiss.

"Shoo now, Mister! Yer always expectin' a *certain* send-off on Mondays." Patty had a twinkle in her eyes and her skin colored as she waved him away.

"Not this Monday. No time. I have to get goin'. Chuck's waitin'. But one more taste for the road won't hurt."

Before Patty could protest, Robert pulled her close, his hand firm around her waist and kissed her with a passion that left her breathless. As he strode out of the room with a satisfied grin, he couldn't help but savor the rare moment of leaving his wife utterly speechless.

* * *

The bells jingled above the doorway as Robert stepped into Fancy's Mercantile. Behind the counter, Fanny was ringing up a customer. She glanced up and greeted Robert with a warm smile.

"Well, there ya are, Mr. Clark! I've been waitin' for ya!" she said, pulling two neatly wrapped packages from under her counter.

At the same time Shirley Conlin, Patty's good friend, picked up her purchased items and turned around to see whom Fanny was talking to. "Robert, what are ya doin' here instead of turnin' wrenches?" she teased, her tone light.

A guilty look washed over Robert's face. The Conlins had been close friends for years, and the last thing he needed was Shirley accidentally letting something slip to Patty.

Clearing his throat, Robert glanced around quickly before leaning in closer. "Well, I'm doin' a little shoppin' for Patty," he admitted in a low voice. "So, I'd be much obliged if y'all didn't mention seein' me here today."

Shirley's eyes twinkled as she grinned knowingly. "Not a word!" she promised, giving a gesture of zipping her lips. Then, resting a hand on Robert's arm, she added with a soft chuckle, "Y'all know with me, Robert, ya can take it to the bank."

Robert smiled, reassured. With Shirley and her husband Billy, he knew this to be true. He could trust them with anything. Now, had it been Ida Mae standing at the counter, he'd be nervous.

Letting out a breath of relief, Robert nodded. "Thanks, Shirley." As she made her way to the door, he added, "be sure and tell Billy hello for me. After the holidays and the weddin' the four of us need to get together and play some cards again."

"We'd love that. Somethin' to look forward to in the new year," Shirley replied with a smile.

Then, her expression grew serious. "But Robert, don't think I'll be so nice then."

* * *

Tuesday, December 13th, 1966

Jessie May decided to stop by James's place on her way to work. She hadn't seen him since Saturday, and *Light up Cordova* had been a whirlwind of fun and festive activities. Between time spent with Karen Norraine and Betty Lou, watching the band, and hanging out with the group afterward, she'd barely spoken with James. She hadn't even had the chance to ask what he thought of their first gig. She'd already told him how good she thought it was, but she wanted to hear his thoughts and to tell him how proud she was of him. So, she decided on a quick surprise visit before heading to work.

She knocked on the front door and was surprised when Rita answered.

Equally startled, Rita greeted her with a warm smile. "Well, Jessie May! I didn't know ya were comin' this mornin'. Come on in. I just got home from the bakery. I'm on my lunch break. Ya eaten yet?"

"Yes, but thank ya kindly for the offer. I don't have much time as I'm headin' to the school right after this," Jessie replied politely. "I sure appreciate the offer, though."

"Yer welcome. I suppose yer lookin' for James."

"Yes, ma'am," Jessie May answered, stepping inside and following Rita toward the kitchen. "We haven't really talked since Saturday night, and I'm dyin' to know how he thought things went at Linny's."

"Well, I'll have to go wake him for ya, so you can ask him."

Jessie glanced at the clock on the wall above the sink. It was eleven o'clock on the dot. *That's strange*, she thought. *James is still in bed?*

"Said he has a headache," Rita explained, catching the puzzled look on Jessie's face.

"Oh no, is he sick?" Her voice was laced with concern.

"I don't think so," Rita answered. "He was out with Hank Timball last night."

"Oh? I thought he was out with the guys," Jessie said, a note of confusion in her voice.

"No, he told me they were busy. But he ran into Hank Saturday night, and they made plans to get together. I think they needed to…ya know…support each other."

Jessie nodded solemnly. That was tough to think about. A war halfway around the world still had its grip on them. They had left Vietnam, but Vietnam hadn't left them.

With a slight smile, Jessie said softly, "Thanks for lettin' me know, Rita. I appreciate it. On second thought, maybe we shouldn't wake him."

"Nah, you'll be good medicine. I'll run up and stir him. Then I best get goin'." Rita glanced at the clock. "Heavens to Betsy, I don't have much time before I gotta get back. This time of year, the bakery is a madhouse." Rita let out an exasperated breath.

"I bet it is," Jessie said sympathetically. "And I'm sure it doesn't help havin' to make all the

43

caramels for our weddin' on top of the regular holiday craziness!"

"Jessie May, don't ya dare feel bad about that." Rita said warmly, her voice full of reassurance. "It's my honor to be makin' those caramels for yer weddin'. If ya hadn't asked me...well, then I really *would* be exhausted...from gettin' my feathers all ruffled that you *didn't* ask." She chuckled. "So don't give it another thought. I'll go wake James, and then I'm scootin' out the front door. I'll say my good-bye now. Have a good day at work."

She gave Jessie a quick hug, grabbed what was left of her sandwich from the plate on the table, and hustled to go wake James.

* * *

Jessie sat at the kitchen table, her thoughts racing. She was sure James had told her he was going out with Nathaniel, RJ, and Bobby Ray last night. Maybe he hadn't wanted her to know he was with Hank. He tried hard not to talk about Vietnam with her, and Hank was part of Vietnam. Knowing James, he probably didn't want to make her worry.

Yet here she was, worrying anyway.

Heavenly Father, I cast my anxiety on You. Help me not to be anxious. Give me yer peace that transcends all understandin' and guard my heart and my mind. Amen.

She heard the front door shut. Rita was heading back to the bakery. Jessie sucked in a breath and held it, nerves fluttering, as she waited for James. She didn't have to wait long. Within a minute, he stepped into the kitchen, squinting against the light.

44

His dark hair was a tousled mess, sticking up in front, a far cry from the uniform high-and-tight military cut he'd had when he first came home. It had grown out a lot since October, and Jessie had always loved his hair. And his eyes.

Those familiar dark eyes, still heavy with sleep, landed on her. Then came a slow, lazy smile. "Jessie?" he croaked, his voice raspy from sleep. He ran a quick hand through his hair. "Butter my backside and call me a biscuit, Mama didn't say *you* were here. She just told me to get my buns downstairs. Didn't say why. I wish she'd told me to brush my teeth first."

Jessie giggled as James crossed the room and wrapped her in a hug. He was still warm, his skin lingering with the heat of sleep. Tilting his head down, he pressed a soft kiss to her lips.

"James Theodore!" she laughed, wrinkling her nose as she pulled back. "You do need a toothbrush!"

"I don't doubt that," James chuckled, tightening his arms around her. "This is a nice surprise, but what are ya doin' here? Don't ya have to work?"

"I've got a little time. I came in early so I could stop by and see you. We haven't really talked since yer gig Saturday night, and I've been dyin' to know what ya thought of it." She paused, then frowned slightly. "But first, why were ya still in bed?"

James caught the concern in her voice and gently guided her to the table. "Let's sit." They settled side by side, and he took both of her hands in his. "I was just worn out. John had me choppin' wood

45

all day yesterday and it takes me two times as long with my darn shoulder. Said he wanted the winter stash stocked up. Pretty sure I chopped enough to heat all of Walker County." He winced, rubbing his shoulder. "And now I'm sore to boot."

"James," Jessie said, alarmed. "Should ya be doin' that with...ya know...yer injury?"

"The doc said I can do things as tolerated. And honestly, it felt good, Jess. I need to be movin' again," he said, reassuring her. "But holy smokes, I'm outta shape. That woodpile kicked my butt."

Relief washed over Jessie. "Ah. That explains it."

"Explains what?" he asked, raising an eyebrow.

"Nothin'." She quickly dismissed her concern, brushing off her earlier worry. "So, how'd ya think yer band's first night went?"

James's face lit up. "Well...if Linny askin' us to play again means anythin'!"

"Oh, James!" Jessie squealed, throwing her arms around him.

"Ooo, I like that," he teased, dipping his head to nuzzle her neck.

"James Theodore!" She squirmed away, giggling. "Uh-uh-uh!" Jessie wagged her finger at him. "I told ya...you need a toothbrush!" She smoothed her blouse, eyeing him with mock sternness. "Besides, I can't get my clothes wrinkled or hair mussed. I'm headin' to work."

James hung his head in a dramatic gesture of defeat.

"However," she said, a coy look on her face, "I *might* be persuaded to allow a good-bye kiss…provided it's minty fresh."

James shot to his feet and bolted down the hallway without another word.

"James!" she called after him. "Where are ya goin'? I don't have much time. I gotta leave in five minutes!"

His voice floated back from the bathroom, muffled by the distance. "This operation now requires toothpaste and possibly a little mouthwash. Don't rush greatness!"

Jessie rolled her eyes, laughing as she stood and pushed in her chair. She crossed her arms and tapped her fingers impatiently on her forearm. "Well, greatness has four minutes, so shake a leg! This gal's gotta clock in soon or I'll be answerin' to Mrs. Penderlyn, and I'm a little too old to be written up for bein' tardy!"

* * *

Jessie pulled open the front door to the school, instantly taking in the scent of waxed floors mingling with the faint smell of chalk dust. A smile tugged at the corners of her mouth, her thoughts were still lingering on James. Entering the office, she spotted Mrs. Penderlyn standing on her trusty stepstool, reaching up to file something in the cabinet. "Good afternoon, Mrs. Penderlyn," Jessie called out cheerfully.

Startled, Mrs. Penderlyn flinched, clutching the cabinet for balance. "Land sakes, child! Ya need to forewarn me better before hollerin' while I'm up here!" she exclaimed, stepping down from her perch

47

with an exaggerated huff. At barely five feet tall, Mrs. Penderlyn relied on that stool for nearly everything. She adjusted her perfectly coiffed beehive as she turned to Jessie, her face softening.

"Now that yer here, I need a word with ya before I go. I'm glad ya arrived a little early, even if ya scared me half to death."

"Mrs. Penderlyn, I've been arrivin' at this same time every Tuesday and Thursday for a year now," Jessie clarified, humor tinging her words. "Y'all should know I'm comin'!"

Mrs. Penderlyn narrowed her eyes. "Now, don't go gettin' smarter than yer britches...or I might just keep my surprise to myself," she said, revealing a little smile.

"Oh? A surprise? What would that be? I love surprises."

Before answering, Mrs. Penderlyn tilted her head in a way she always did when something was on her mind. It often struck Jessie's funny bone. She had to turn away to keep from giggling. Every time Mrs. Penderlyn did that, it looked like she was going to tip over from the weight of her beehive.

"Everythin' okay, Jessie May?" Mrs. Penderlyn stepped forward out of concern, a crease forming on her forehead.

Jessie cleared her throat. "Yes, Ma'am, just a little tickle, and I thought I heard somethin' out in the hall. But I'm sure it was nothin'. Go ahead. What about that surprise?" She turned to face Mrs. Penderlyn, doing her best to keep a straight face.

"Clara Sue's twins just turned a year old in November, and now she's expectin' again. I reckon Tuesday and Thursday afternoons just ain't gonna be enough anymore." A mix of excitement and pride was obvious in her voice. "She's gonna need more help, and I'd like more time with my grandbabies."

Suddenly, Mrs. Penderlyn wore a smile the size of a watermelon.

Jessie couldn't keep it in any longer. Mrs. Penderlyn looked too darn cute. Letting out a little chuckle, she offered her sincere congratulations. "Oh, Mrs. Penderlyn! I am just so happy for you! That is plumb wonderful news! I can't believe Clara Sue is expectin' again!"

"I know! Her husband is beyond excited. He's like a dog with two tails. But Clara Sue is kinda nervous. With the twins just bein' a year old and all, she knows she'll have her hands full. That's why they're goin' to need a little more help."

Mrs. Penderlyn reached up and grabbed the ever-present pencil tucked into her beehive and began jotting down something on a sheet of paper. The soft scratching of graphite filled the quiet office space as Jessie waited, uncertain whether to speak or let Mrs. Penderlyn finish.

After a moment, Mrs. Penderlyn handed her the note. "I am givin' this to Mr. Bieberdorf today. I would like ya to work full days Tuesdays and Thursdays, at least for now, with the potential for more later. How's that sound?"

Jessie blinked in surprise, her heart racing. Full days? This was more than she'd hoped for. She couldn't wait to tell James. What a happy new year this would be. Visions of her and James's future danced in her mind. With her daddy talking to James about working at the shop, and now this steady schedule for her, everything seemed to be falling perfectly into place.

"Land sakes, Jessie May!" Mrs. Penderlyn interrupted her thoughts. "Ya just gonna stand there grinnin' like a mule eatin' briars, or ya gonna give me the answer I am hopin' that smile means?"

"Yes, ma'am!" Jessie exclaimed. "I would love to work full days on Tuesdays and Thursdays."

"Now don't go gettin' too excited just yet," Mrs. Penderlyn cautioned. "We need Mr. Bieberdorf and Mr. Haugen to approve the change first, and they will have to run it by the school board."

"Thank you so much for thinkin' of me," Jessie graciously responded, though her mind was already looking ahead to what this meant for their future.

* * *

Jessie couldn't wait to tell James about her conversation with Mrs. Penderlyn. The new year was proving promising for both of them…James at Chuck's with her father and Jessie increasing her hours at the school. Thinking about their future, Jessie's mind raced with the excitement. The year was going to bring many exciting changes. Changes as Mr. and Mrs. James Patterson. A huge smile spread across her face as she thought about the happy new year ahead.

On her way home after work, Jessie decided to stop again at James's house. The good news just couldn't wait. Correction—*she* couldn't wait.

When she walked up to the front door around 3:40, she figured as busy as December was, Rita would still be at the bakery, and she knew John

50

wouldn't be home from Fleck's Insurance yet. They'd have the place to themselves, which was exactly what she hoped. She wanted only James to hear the news first.

Jessie rang the doorbell and listened as it chimed inside. Shortly after, James opened the door. His dark brown eyes locked onto hers, making her heart flutter. His hair had been combed since she'd seen him that morning. He looked so handsome standing there. She instantly smiled.

James returned her smile with a rather teasing one. "Ya look happy as a clam at high tide."

"I am!" She stepped inside. "Yer parents home yet?" she asked, knowing the answer.

"No, why?" James cocked an eyebrow. "Ya hopin' for a little more than this mornin's kiss?"

"James Theodore!" she exclaimed, barely pretending to push him away as he pulled her into his arms. Unsuccessful with her attempt, she melted into his embrace. It felt so good being close to him, she almost forgot why she'd stopped by in the first place. Shaking her head slightly, she looked up at him, meeting his gaze. "I have some good news to share with you, and I wanted ya to be the first to hear it."

"Let's go sit in the livin' room. I was just workin' on writin' a new song."

They walked into the cozy room. James picked up his guitar from the couch and leaned it against the bookcase, then patted the cushion beside him. Jessie sat down, and he took her hand gently in his.

"Alright," he said, smiling. "I'm all ears."

Jessie immediately launched into the story, practically bubbling with giddiness as she explained

51

how Clara Sue was expecting again and Mrs. Penderlyn wanted to spend more time helping with her grandbabies. She told him Mrs. Penderlyn asked her to work full days on Tuesdays and Thursdays starting in January right after they got back from their honeymoon. The schedule was perfect. It was just enough to help with expenses as they started out on their own, but not too much so that she couldn't keep up their household.

She barely paused for a breath, finishing in a rush, "So, what do ya think? You haven't said a word. Aren't ya goin' to say anythin'?"

James closed his eyes and shook his head slightly, a small smirk playing on his lips. She hadn't given him a chance to say a word. When he opened his eyes, she was looking at him intently. He didn't say anything at first, just raised a hand to her face, gently rubbing her soft skin with his thumb. His fingers found a strand of her hair, and he played with it absently.

Finally, he spoke. "I just hope…" he trailed off.

"Yes?" Jessie leaned in closer, hanging on his words.

"I just hope…" he paused again, letting the suspense build.

"Come on now!" she demanded with impatience.

"I hope ya don't start wearin' yer hair in a beehive."

Pulling away, Jessie smacked his arm. "James Theodore, what am I goin' to do with you?"

"Hmmm," he said with a wink, pulling her into his arms again. "I can think of a few things." She laughed as he embraced her, holding her close and soaking in her scent and the sound of her laughter. "All jokin' aside," he murmured into her hair, "congratulations, Jess. What a great way to push into the new year. This is wonderful news for you, Jessie May."

Tilting her head back to meet his eyes, she whispered, "Wonderful news for *us*."

Chapter 4
Tidings of Comfort and Joy

Saturday, December 17ᵗʰ, 1966

"Well, don't you look all snuggled in," Jessie said, easing into Lydia's room and shutting the door with a soft click.

Lydia was curled beneath the covers, a book tucked in her hands. She placed it on her nightstand and sat up. "Ya ready?"

"Sure am," Jessie replied, crossing the room. "Let's scoot yer bed out again so we aren't fightin' yer slanted ceilin'."

Lydia kicked off her quilt and reached for the head of her bed. "You grab that end. Ready? One—two—three!"

Together they slid the bed away from the wall. Lydia opened her nightstand drawer and rummaged through a tangled mess of tapestry needles and crochet hooks. She pulled out a couple nearly finished gifts...a brown stocking cap and one orange mitten, placing its completed match on her pillow.

"Which ya wanna work on?"

"Doesn't matter to me," Jessie replied. "You pick. I'll lock the door, just in case."

"I'll take the mitten." Lydia flopped back down and got right to work.

Jessie grabbed the cap and sat at the foot of the bed. "Daddy's gonna love this. Anythin' in his Cleveland Browns colors is a win. I wasn't sure we'd finish in time, but we're almost done."

She looked up to see Lydia nodding in agreement. For a moment, she just watched her sister, struck by how much she was growing up. At sixteen, Lydia no longer looked like a little girl. She wore makeup now, the soft ivory of her cheeks dusted with a delicate rose blush. Half her hair was pulled back with a ribbon, the rest tumbling over her shoulders in loose curls.

"Yer real pretty, ya know that?" she said, her voice warm with affection.

Lydia blinked and waved off the compliment. "Mercy, what's gotten into you?"

"I mean it, Lydia Ruth. Yer blushin' like a peach in the summer sun, but just take the compliment."

Lydia shrugged, a little bashful. "Aint' used to hearin' that kinda thing. What's gotten into you?"

Jessie smiled softly. "Just hit me. My little sister ain't my *little* sister anymore."

Lydia rolled her eyes. "Now, don't go gettin' emotional on me. Mama's been doin' enough of that."

They both laughed.

"She has been, hasn't she?" Jessie agreed, reaching to grab the scissors. "I reckon one day we'll be the ones tearin' up when our babies start gettin' grown." She snipped the yarn, leaving a long tail to finish the top of the cap. "So, whatcha readin'?" she asked, tilting her head toward the nightstand.

"*Fifteen* by Beverly Clearly. Got it for my birthday last year. It's about a girl named Jane who babysits, meets this older guy named Stan…and she thinks she's too ordinary for him to notice her."

Jessie eyed her curiously. "So…do you ever dream of havin' a boyfriend?"

"Jessie May!" Lydia's cheeks instantly flushed a deep shade of pink.

"Well," Jessie teased, "I didn't know if ya were desribin' Jane's story or yers."

"Just 'cause you've got weddin' bells chimin' doesn't mean I do."

"True," Jessie said, still smiling at her sister. "But it wasn't long ago you said makeup was a bother and boys were just plain gross. And now, look at ya. Yer beautiful."

"Okay, new subject." Lydia quickly diverted the topic. "What time should we leave for carolin'?"

Jessie shook her head and rolled her eyes, acknowledging the change of subject. "Pastor Mark said to meet at First Baptist 'round 6:45, so we can start singin' by 7:00. Should we leave at 6:30, just to be safe?"

Lydia nodded. "Sounds good. Then I can meet up with Mary."

Mary Bustad had been Lydia's best friend ever since she moved to Cordova a couple years back, during eighth grade. From the first day, the two had been inseparable sharing secrets, favorite books, and just about everything in between.

"There. Done." Jessie held up the brown stocking cap.

"Perfect timin'!" Lydia grinned, raising the orange mitten. A sudden knock at the door startled her. She quickly grabbed both mittens and instinctively tucked them under her pillow. "Who is it?" she anxiously called.

"Yer daddy," came Robert's muffled voice. "Yer mama says it's time to eat. She wants to eat early so y'all aren't late for carolin'."

"We'll be down in a minute," Lydia answered hastily.

"Jessie May in there too?"

"Yes, Daddy."

"What're y'all up to in there?"

"Nothin' ya need worryin' 'bout, Daddy," Jessie replied with a grin. "Unless ya want a lump o' coal for Christmas!"

He chuckled. "Well, ya might get coal from yer mama if her supper gets cold."

"Yes, sir," they chimed together.

* * *

Robert was chuckling to himself as he pushed through the swinging door into the kitchen.

"What'r ya laughin' 'bout?" Patty asked, oven mitts on both hands as she carried a steaming casserole dish of sweet potatoes. "Hold the door for me, please." As she passed through, she added, "Did ya tell Jessie May and Lydia Ruth it's time to eat?"

"I did," Robert replied, still grinning. "I think those two are up to somethin'."

Patty smiled, raising her eyebrows knowingly. "Well, it *is* Christmas time, Robert." She set the casserole down on the trivet at the center of the dining table. Brushing a loose strand of hair from her face, she turned back toward the kitchen.

She slid by Robert on her way back into the kitchen. "Carrie Grace, can ya bring the sweet tea out to the table, please?" Back by the stove, she picked up the large serving dish and began ladling chicken and dumplings from the frying pan. The rich, hearty aroma filled the air, warm and savory.

Robert, still standing by the door, nudged it open once more as she spun around with the dish in hand.

"Would ya grab the cornbread?" she asked.

"Yes, ma'am," he replied, giving her a little pat on the backside as she passed.

"Hey now!" Patty laughed, sidestepping with practiced ease. "Don't make me drop our supper." She set the chicken and dumplings down with care, then looked up. "Where are those girls?"

As if on cue, Jessie and Lydia came bounding into the room.

"Whatcha need us to do, Mama?" Jessie asked, chipper as ever.

"Just grab the napkins and we'll be ready to sit up." Patty eased into her chair with a long sigh.

Carrie Grace followed in with the tea, setting it on the table. Jessie tugged open the drawer of the mahogany sideboard where they kept their everyday napkins, just like Grandma Williams used to. She grabbed five napkins, the soft pressed cotton a scented mix of lavender and old wood, and placed one at each setting.

"Let's all sit up, shall we?" Robert said, pulling out his chair. "Time for grace."

The girls took their seats, reaching across the table to clasp hands. In quiet unison, they bowed their heads to pray.

Robert began, his voice steady and heartfelt. "Dear Heavenly Father, we thank thee, Lord, for this good food and for the hands that prepared it." He gave Patty's hand a gentle squeeze. "Thank ya for the comfort of our home and the joy that fills it. Lord, I'm mighty grateful to be surrounded by my family, watchin' my girls grow into fine young women. As we prepare to celebrate the birth of yer son, keep our hearts humble and focused on Him. Thank ya, for the good news we receive with the comin' of our Savior. Good tidings, indeed, of comfort and joy. Bless this meal to nourish our bodies and bless us to yer service. In yer holy name we pray. Amen."

As always, he ended the prayer with a squeeze to Patty and Jessie's hands before letting go. "Now, let's eat. I'm hungry as a bear in spring." He winked at Carrie. "Looks wonderful, Pats."

The dishes were passed and while food filled the bellies, cheerful conversation filled the room. Robert sat back and watched his girls with a quiet smile, listening to their chatter. Their laughter sang in harmony around the room like an old familiar hymn. His gaze settled on Jessie May, seated beside him. In exactly two weeks, she'd become a bride and that chair would be empty. His little girl, the one who first made him a father, would be at a table of her own. In a home of her own.

James's wife.

He let that sink in. Let it sting a little.

"Robert?"

Patty's voice broke through his thoughts.

"Huh? Yes?" he blinked.

"Can ya please pass the sweet potatoes?" she asked, enunciating each word for emphasis. "I've

59

only asked ya three times. Yer sittin' there like a calf starin' at a new gate."

"Sorry, darlin'," Robert apologized, handing her the dish. "I was just thinkin' how blessed I am. Thankful for y'all." He noticed Patty's eyes beginning to glisten, and added quickly, "And y'all know what else I am thankful for?"

Patty shook her head, grabbing her napkin to dab a stray tear.

"Dessert," Robert declared. "A little birdie told me ya made banana puddin'."

Carrie Grace perked up. "Not just Mama! I helped. I sliced the bananas and crushed the wafers, and I whipped the cream all by myself!"

"Well, I'm ready if anyone else is. That is, unless you girls are too *busy* to have dessert?" Robert goaded, eyeing Jessie and Lydia.

"Coal, remember, Daddy?" Lydia teasingly reminded him.

"Now wait a minute! I was only doin' what yer mama told me. Gettin' y'all to the table. If I hadn't…" He dropped his voice, an impish grin on his face. "Worse than coal. I'd face her wrath!"

"Robert Christopher!" Patty exclaimed, playing along. "You keep that up, mister, and ya might just get coal for Christmas…and nothin' for dessert."

"Whoa now," he said, feigning alarm. "Let's not get hasty. No need for things to get ugly." He winked at his girls, then leaned back in his chair.

"Robert, I know good and well ya can't go without my cookin'. Especially dessert. If I didn't know the way to yer heart is through yer stomach, half my to-do list wouldn't get done." She glanced around the table at the girls and then flashed a victorious grin at her husband.

Robert turned toward Jessie. "Well, Jessie May, there ya have it, the secret to a good marriage."

Jessie looked at him, eyes bright with curiosity.

He tried not to smile, but it crept in anyhow. "What yer mama just described…some folks might call that *manipulation*. But me? I prefer to call it *sweet incentive*."

* * *

Jessie and Lydia made their way through the crowd in front of First Baptist.

"I see James!" Jessie announced, her voice bright with excitement. He was standing with RJ and Landa Jane, Bobby Ray and Janet, and Nathaniel. The sight of him always made her heart flutter. "Let's go stand by them. Mary will find ya." She grabbed Lydia's hand and pulled her along eagerly.

"Hey, y'all!" She waved as they approached the group.

The gang greeted Jessie and Lydia. James came over right away, pulling her into a warm hug. Nathaniel stepped aside next to Lydia as if the pairs were pushing him out of the circle.

"Guess it's a couple's night," he teased, giving Lydia's shoulder a playful bump.

Bashfully, Lydia looked down, suddenly feeling self-conscious. Nathaniel stared at her. Lydia Ruth looked different tonight. There was a subtle change, something new that he couldn't put his finger on.

She glanced back up at him, her eyes slowly meeting his. Her hair hung down over her wool coat and was topped with a red knit stocking cap, making her dark brown hair more breathtaking than he'd even seen. The dark navy color of her coat complimented her ivory complexion, drawing attention to her captivating eyes.

Nathaniel couldn't help but stare.

"What?" she asked, breaking the awkward silence.

"Nothin'," Nathaniel responded, shrugging off the awkward moment. "Ya look really nice tonight, Lydia Ruth."

Uncertain how to respond, Lydia offered a small, appreciative smile. The strange moment was thankfully interrupted when Mary suddenly appeared.

"Hey, I thought that was you over here," Mary smiled, looking around at the rest of the group. "I'm ready for some carolin'!"

A wave of excitement rippled through the group. The mood was energetic and everyone fell into the rhythm of the evening. Arlette's voice could be heard, rising above the crowd as she tried to gather everyone in for final instructions.

* * *

Nathaniel couldn't quite reconcile his thoughts. He was looking at Jessie May's younger sister, but he wasn't seeing a little sister anymore. She looked like a young woman. She looked…beautiful.

A jab to the ribs snapped him out of it.

"Ya woolgatherin' or what?" Bobby Ray teased, his tone pointed.

Nathaniel coughed, scrambling to recover. Thankfully, Bobby had no clue what he'd actually been thinking. "Nah," he said quickly, throwing on a grin. "I was just wonderin' if Janet's gettin' sick of ya yet?"

Bobby slugged him in the arm.

"Ouch!" Nathaniel yelped, rubbing the spot, though he was still smirking.

Bobby chuckled but leaned in a moment later, lowering his voice. He cupped his hand near his mouth and whispered, serious now, "I don't wanna mess this one up."

Nathaniel's grin softened. He met his friend's eyes, a quiet understanding passing between them. Bobby Ray had changed, and he could see it clear as day.

He stole one more glance at Lydia, who was now chatting with Mary, unaware.

Yes, things were changing.

* * *

What just happened? Lydia blinked, heat creeping up her neck. The night air was cold against her cheeks, but a sudden warmth flushed through her chest. Her stomach fluttered. She gave her head a little shake, trying to brush off the odd feeling. *Get a grip.* She'd clearly been reading too much *Fifteen.* She was likening herself to Jane and Nathaniel to Stan.

She glanced quickly at Nathaniel. Thankfully, he wasn't looking her way. He was a lot like Stan. Older. More sure of himself. And, mercy, so good looking. A soft sigh escaped her lips before she could stop it.

Mary's laughter pulled her attention away from Nathaniel.

"I'm so excited to go carolin'!" Mary gushed, practically bouncing with eagerness. "Do ya think Johnny will be here?"

Mary had a big crush on Johnny Reynolds. He was tall, freckled, a year older than they were, and had been the center of Mary's attention since October.

Grateful for the distraction, Lydia answered, "I would guess so. His daddy's on the church board, so I can't imagine him not bein' here tonight."

"Oooooo!" Mary squealed, her eyes dancing. "He's so dreamy."

Lydia couldn't help but laugh, rolling her eyes affectionately. "Yer so dreamy," she teased, grabbing Mary's hand. "Come on, the group's leavin'. We're gonna get left behind."

* * *

The night was drawing to a close. They were just stopping at one last house. Pastor Mark and Arlette, at the front of the group, stepped up to ring the doorbell. Old man Higgins answered the door, wearing a matted terry cloth robe, the stubble of the day's growth shadowing his face. He rubbed his chin and squinted.

The group gathered on the porch, ready to sing the final Christmas carol of the evening as the old man stood in his doorway, a small smile beginning to show on his weathered face. The carolers' voices filled the chilly air as they launched into the song Arlette had selected for their closing carol:

God rest ye merry gentlemen
Let nothing you dismay
Remember Christ our Savior
Was born on Christmas Day.

Nathaniel glanced over his shoulder, his gaze lingering on Lydia. Singing, she looked angelic. He shook his head, trying to shake away his distracting thoughts. What was happening to him? A feeling stirred inside him, unfamiliar yet comforting. A feeling that was subtle, but undeniable joy.

Oh, tidings of comfort and joy
Comfort and joy
Oh, tidings of comfort and joy.

Chapter 5
The Best Gift of All

Tuesday, December 20th, 1966

Lydia and Carrie stepped into the school office just as Jessie glanced up from her desk. Lydia had picked up Carrie from the elementary school and timed it right to meet Jessie as she got off work. The three of them were headed out to shop for Patty's Christmas gift.

Carrie lit up the room with her bright voice. "Howdy, Jessie! Ya ready to shop for Mama's Christmas present?"

"I can't believe we don't have one for her yet," Lydia said, her tone tinged with disappointment.

"I know," Jessie agreed, straightening the last of her papers from the desk she shared with Mrs. Penderlyn. "Between weddin' plans, school and work schedules, and all the extra holiday festivities, it's been nearly impossible for the three of us to sneak away together." Jessie sighed, knowing deep down that tallying excuses wouldn't lessen the guilt she felt.

Scooting around the main counter, Jessie flicked off the lights and took Carrie's hand. "Okay, where to first? Hank's Hardware or Fancy's?" She looked between Lydia and Carrie, waiting for their vote.

66

"I say we head to Hank's," Lydia suggested after a moment of thought. "I'm guessin' we can find a new kitchen timer there."

"Oooo, good idea, Lydia Ruth!" Carrie chimed in, practically bouncing. "Mama was hintin' to Daddy the other day that she needed one."

"And, I know Daddy didn't get her one," Jessie added as they stepped out into the cold. "He bought her somethin' else."

"What is it?" Carrie asked, her insatiable curiosity animating her face.

"Never ya mind, little miss." Lydia playfully tapped the tip of Carrie's nose. "Yer not exactly known for keepin' secrets."

"Yes, I am!" Carrie insisted indignantly.

"Oh, really?" Lydia arched a brow. "Like the time ya told Daddy durin' supper about the wheelbarrow Mama got him for his birthday? Right after she went to all that trouble sneakin' it home and hidin' it in the shed?"

Carrie wilted. "Oh," she muttered, her shoulders sinking.

Jessie tousled Carrie's hair affectionately. "And now it's one of Daddy's favorite birthday memories," she said warmly. "So, pick that chin up. Let's go find the perfect gift for Mama."

At Hank's, they found a timer to replace Patty's old one, which always got stuck when it wound down to the end. At Fancy's, they picked out a cheerful dish towel set in avocado green and mustard yellow, decorated with little daisies. Across the center, embroidered in neat, looping stitches, were the words: *Happiness is Homemade*. They all agreed it was very fitting for their mother and would go nicely with the timer.

Feeling rather pleased with their purchases, the trio began walking home.

"Y'all know," Carrie said, skipping a little between her sisters, "this is gonna be one of our last walks together as sisters before ya get hitched, Jessie May."

Jessie stifled a laugh. "Why on earth would ya say it like that? We'll still be sisters."

"I mean walkin' *home* together," Carrie clarified, her expression pensive. "You'll go to yer own home after the weddin' and be with James. Then Lydia will prob'ly leave next. And then…" Her voice trailed off as she somberly stared down at the path.

Jessie stopped, gently turning Carrie to face her. "No matter where we live or when we marry, we'll always be yer big sisters. That's not changin', okay?" She placed her hand over Carrie's heart. "Home is where the heart is and we'll be right here with ya."

Carrie blinked up at Jessie, her eyes shimmering with emotion. "Really?"

"Really," Jessie reassured her, taking one of Carrie's hands in her own.

"And don't ever forget," Lydia added, reaching for Carrie's other hand, "you can pick yer husband, but ya can't pick your sisters. So yer stuck with us, little miss."

Carrie giggled, her worry melting into contentment. The three of them continued walking, their shoes crunching over the frosty gravel of their driveway as their house came into view. She chattered happily about how Mama would react to their gifts, which she promised to keep a secret.

At that, Jessie and Lydia shared a quiet smile.

Hand-in-hand, they casually strolled the rest of the way home, listening to Carrie's prattle. Even with so much ahead of them, moments like this were a reminder that some things, like being family, never change.

* * *

Thursday, December 22nd, 1966

It was the last day of school before Christmas break. Both Mrs. Penderlyn and Jessie were working that day. Mrs. Penderlyn had planned to walk Jessie through the extra responsibilities she'd be taking on after the holidays. She had agreed, or rather insisted, Jessie come in to observe the morning routine and learn how everything was done.

After Christmas break, Jessie would begin working full days on Tuesdays and Thursdays. But since school resumed on January 3rd and James and Jessie would still be on their honeymoon, Mrs. Penderlyn assured her she'd cover that first week. After that, starting January 10th, she expected Jessie ready to step in fully. "Prepared to meet all of Mr. Bieberdorf's expectations," she'd told Jessie. Though Jessie was beginning to realize those expectations were more Mrs. Penderlyn's.

Once they'd checked everything off the competency list, they wrapped things up in the office for the holiday break. Mrs. Penderlyn wished Jessie a Merry Christmas, and Jessie returned the sentiment before bundling into her coat and scarf. She planned to walk over to James's before heading home. He'd mentioned on the phone last night that Elizabeth and David, his sister and brother-in-law, were arriving today.

Ever since David left his job at the steel mill for a teaching position at the University of Alabama Medical Center, his schedule had become more flexible. He had worked at the mill until a position at the university opened. He now taught anatomy and physiology to medical and pharmacy students at UAMC. Jessie smiled, thinking of how well he was doing for their family, even if it was just the two of them. They did not want children, and Jessie understood why. Having been forced into the role of "mother" after their daddy died, not only caring for James but for their own mama, Elizabeth had long ago lost any desire to become one herself.

The walk to James's house wasn't far, but Jessie tugged her scarf higher around her neck as she stepped out the front doors of the school. The brisk air sent a shiver through her. She hadn't told James she'd be stopping by, but the thought of seeing her soon-to-be sister a little early filled her with eager anticipation.

The plan was for her to spend tomorrow with James's family, Christmas Eve on Saturday with hers, and then on Christmas Day they'd agreed on spending with their own families. Next year, that would change. They would need to start alternating holidays between both sides. But for now, they wanted one last year of tradition before they began splitting holidays…before becoming Mr. and Mrs. Patterson.

Jessie quickened her pace as the cool breeze sent goosebumps up her legs. Her long plaid wool

70

skirt offered little protection against the breeze going through her thin nylons, but it wasn't long before she was standing in front of James's front door. She rang the bell, a confident grin spreading across her face. She was ready for this next chapter, even if it meant dividing holidays. The thought of starting new traditions and having a place of their own made her almost giddy with excitement. A sigh escaped. She blinked with a little disbelief. *They would have a home of their own.*

Mr. Clarkson, their future landlord, had said they could start moving things in the first part of next week. A flutter of butterflies swirled in Jessie's stomach at the thought. She laughed to herself. *We don't even have that much to move in.*

She and James would be renting the little yellow house on Brummel Street, right behind Fleck's Insurance on the south end of Main. John, James's stepdad, had teased them about its location, joking that he would be able to keep an eye on them from his office window.

Jessie didn't mind. She liked the idea of help being close by if they ever needed it.

Just then, the front door swung open with a gust, snapping Jessie out of her thoughts. Elizabeth's face lit up the moment she saw her.

"My sister!" she exclaimed, pulling Jessie into an exuberant hug that nearly squeezed the air out of her.

"Soon-to-be," Jessie corrected, her voice laced with amusement, though it was muffled against Elizabeth's shoulder.

"What?" Elizabeth teased. "Aren't ya ready for me to be yer sister yet?" Stepping back, she added with a wink, "I know we Pattersons can take some gettin' used to."

Jessie laughed. "I didn't just fall off the turnip truck!" With Elizabeth's arm draped around her, she stepped into the warmth of the house and asked, "So, when did y'all get in?"

"We just barely beat ya here," Elizabeth replied, closing the door with a firm push to ensure it clicked shut. "David had to teach a couple classes this mornin', but now he's off until the 9th. Classes start on the 9th, so he'll prob'ly go back in on the 3rd. First year teachin'...he's still figurin' it all out. It's a lot of work right now." Looping her arm through Jessie's, she led her to the kitchen.

"I bet," Jessie nodded. "But does he like it?"

"Why don't ya ask him yerself!" Elizabeth suggested as they entered the kitchen, where David quickly stood from the table to greet Jessie.

"Jessie!" he greeted, her name garbled by one of Rita's caramels.

"Ya aren't eatin' up our weddin' stash, are ya?" Jessie teased, embracing David in a hug.

Rita jumped into the conversation, "Oh no, I have *those* caramels hidden and locked away or there'd be none left!" Rita shot an amused convicting glance towards David.

"Hey now!" David protested. "I'm not that bad, am I?"

Rita didn't answer. She merely glanced at the nearly empty dish of caramels beside David. They all followed her gaze.

"Alright, maybe I have a little bit of a sweet tooth," David admitted, trying to defend himself.

"A *little* bit?" Elizabeth teased, a smile twitching at the corners of her mouth.

With humor written on his face, he tried to change topics. "I'm feelin' a bit outnumbered, so when does John get home?"

"Not soon enough to have any caramels, that's for sure!" Rita's laughter filled the room. "And David, self-commiseration does not work in this house! I learned that long ago!"

Jessie glanced at her future mother-in-law. Rita's face revealed no sadness, only contented joy and resolve. Her strength and faith were inspiring, and Jessie felt grateful to be gaining such an admirable mother-in-law. To endure what she did when James's father, Bennett, was diagnosed with pancreatic cancer, to watch him suffer and then lose him…Jessie shuddered.

But looking at Rita now, the peace and strength radiating from her, Jessie was awestruck. Rita had endured hardship and emerged stronger. Jessie felt so thankful for the mother she was gaining in Rita. No matter what the future held for her and James, she knew they would have two strong women in their lives supporting them. What a gift. Two amazing mothers. Two incredible blessings.

* * *

Saturday, December 24th, 1966

Jessie had thoroughly enjoyed celebrating Christmas at James's house last night. His Granny Fran, Rita's Mama, was there, along with Rita's sister, Shirley. James told her that his Aunt Shirley never married and spent most holidays with them. Granny Fran brought her signature chocolate-peppermint swirl cookies and even sent some home with Jessie to share.

Jessie loved seeing how James's family celebrated the holiday, especially when they served birthday cake and sang "Happy Birthday" to Jesus. Then, they lit candles and ended with a candlelight rendition of "Silent Night." The lights were dimmed, and the soft glow from the candles bathed the room in a gentle warmth, mixing with the hushed tones of the carol. It felt so intimate.

James explained that they usually did the birthday cake on Christmas Eve, but his mama wanted Jessie to be a part of it, so they'd celebrated early. She had stood beside him, listening to his voice carry the familiar lyrics, feeling like she was in a sweet dream. She loved his voice. When the final notes faded, she'd leaned close and whispered, "I want to keep doin' this when we start our own traditions."

Now, Jessie was eager for James to experience Christmas Eve with her family and join in the Clark family traditions. Celebrating the birth of the Lord was sacred in their home, and one of her favorite moments each year was when her daddy read the story of Jesus' birth from Bible. It was a tradition she hoped to carry on one day with James reading it to their children.

That thought made her smile. Unlike David and Elizabeth, she and James had already talked about wanting kids, but only God new when. She'd learned while James was in Vietnam that His plans weren't always what she had planned. She would have to trust and be patient in His timing.

Patient. Jessie's thoughts halted at that word. Her mama was probably anything but patient right now, wondering where she was. She had tried to be the first one in the bathroom, only to end up behind Lydia who always took forever, thanks to her habit of sneaking books inside. Jessie sighed. While she was standing here woolgathering, she ought to be downstairs helping.

They were having roasted turkey with cornbread dressing and mashed potatoes, and her mama always made a glazed ham to go alongside. Normally, they ate that meal on Christmas day, but Jessie had talked her into switching it to Christmas Eve so James could enjoy it with them. In her opinion, nobody in Alabama made better turkey and cornbread dressing than her mama.

She hustled out of the bathroom and darted across the hall to her bedroom, shutting the door behind her. She yanked open the dresser drawer and pulled out her olive-green sweater. It was a nice choice for Christmas and James liked her in green. After brushing her hair and pulling it into a ponytail, she tossed the brush onto her unmade bed, making a mental note to make it later. Right now, she needed to get downstairs.

Bounding down the steps, she rushed into the kitchen and was pleasantly surprised to find both her sisters helping Patty. Usually, it took several reminders before Carrie came down from her bedroom, but here she was, peeling potatoes. Just as engrossed in a task, Lydia stood beside her also hard at work…an uncommon sight, considering she was often lost in a book and needed a few nudges herself.

The two were giggling over something as they worked. Jessie paused, taking it in. This wasn't just a big year of changes for her. She noticed again how Lydia looked more grown-up. Her hair was parted down the middle and curled at the ends instead of the loose pigtails she used to wear that their daddy called "lazy pigtails". Even Carrie looked older to her today. Her eyes drifted between them. She might be getting married, but they were changing too.

"Ya goin' to just stand there watchin' or ya gonna help?" Patty teased, blowing a stray piece of hair from her face.

"Huh? Oh, sorry, Mama," Jessie laughed. "I was just enjoyin' seein' ya three together."

"Well, ya can admire us while ya work," Patty quipped, turning the corner of her mouth up in a smirk as she wiped her forehead with the back of her hand. "Grab the cornmeal and start makin' the dressin'. The buttermilk's on the counter, Lydia brought in fresh eggs, and the green peppers are already chopped. You'll need to chop the onion."

"I chopped the celery," Carrie added, without looking up.

"Carrie Grace, my, my! Ya really are growin' up," Jessie said, shaking her head as she tied on an apron.

"Yer just noticin' that now?" Carrie scoffed, twirling her wrist dramatically.

Lydia laughed. "Some days, we're not so sure."

Carrie wrinkled her forehead, her brows drawing tight.

"I'm just teasin'," Lydia assured her, patting her back. "You've become pretty handy in the kitchen. I'm impressed."

"Me too," Jessie agreed, cracking an egg into the cornmeal mixture. "Mama won't even miss me when I leave, not with all yer help."

Carrie's shoulders straightened, and she smiled, a mix of satisfaction and pride on her face.

Just then, the back door swung open, and Robert stepped inside, arms full of firewood. "This should fill the log rack for today," he said, nudging the door shut with his foot. He wiped his boots on the rug, lest he earn a scolding from his wife, and paused, inhaling deeply. The aroma within the kitchen was glorious.

Then he looked around. All his girls were working together. This Christmas felt different. Jessie's wedding was just around the corner, and moments like this would become rarer. A soft smile tugged at his lips as he offered up a quiet prayer. *Thank you, Lord, for all the gifts I could ever want, right here before my eyes.*

* * *

James and Robert sat together in the living room while the ladies finished cleaning up in the kitchen. Robert leaned over the side of his chair and grabbed the lever, the footrest of his tan recliner springing up with a well-worn creak. Adjusting his weight, he shifted to get comfortable.

"I'm fuller than a tick on a hound," he groaned, rubbing his stomach. "I prob'ly won't need to eat again 'til the rooster crows tomorrow!" Yawning, he reclined a little more. "Ya know, I think if I lean back like this, my stomach might have a little more room." He closed his eyes.

Before he could drift off, Carrie burst into the room, all energy and excitement. "Daddy, don't go fallin' asleep! It's time to open presents!"

Without opening his eyes, he drawled, "We don't open our presents today. We always wait 'til Christmas Day after the best gift of all has come. And, I don't' mean Santa." He cracked one eye open to peak at her.

Carrie grinned. "Mama says since James is here, we get to open presents early so he doesn't miss out."

James sat up straighter, glancing toward Jessie as she entered the room. "I don't wanna change all yer plans."

"Oh, yer changin' all our plans, alright!" Jessie jumped in the conversation with a wide grin as she plopped down next to him. "At least my plans, anyways." Her eyes locked onto his, and he knew exactly what she meant.

Next Christmas, everything would be different. She would be his wife. Reaching for her hand, James squeezed it gently.

Lydia and Patty soon joined them. Lydia settled in the chair next to the davenport while Patty eased into the oversized gold chair by the bay window. Carrie wasted no time diving under the tree, grabbing packages.

Robert cleared his throat.

Carrie froze mid-reach and turned to him with wide eyes. "Yes, Daddy? Ya want yers first?" she asked, her voice all innocence and anticipation.

Robert raised an eyebrow. "Aren't ya forgettin' somethin', darlin'?"

"Oh!" Carrie quickly grabbed his Bible from under the end table. "The Christmas story!"

Robert reached for the handle of his recliner, lowering the footrest down with a firm *thunk*. Sitting up straight, he took the Bible from Carrie's outstretched hands. The fire crackled, sending shimmers of golden light dancing across the room. Carefully separating the delicate pages, he found his place. He turned his head towards James and explained, "I always like to read this passage from John 1:1-4 before the Christmas story. If we are goin' to truly grasp the gift of Jesus, we need to understand it from the beginnin'."

He paused briefly and then began reading. "In the beginning was the Word, and the Word was with God, and the Word was God. He was with God in the beginning. Through Him all things were made; without Him nothing was made that has been made. In Him was life, and that life was the light of all mankind."

For a moment, Robert looked up and just stared into the glow of the cozy fireplace, transfixed. The wood he had gathered earlier that morning, now burning bright, seemed to add its own touch to the story.

"Christmas is a season of light and life," he said, his voice softer now. "A time to reflect on the miraculous story of Jesus, the Word with God, who entered the world as a child."

"Daddy, aren't ya gonna read from Luke now? I like that part," Carried interrupted.

Robert gave her a patient but pointed look. She stood hushed, fidgeting under his gaze. Patty patted her chair and Carrie went to curl up beside her mama.

"Luke tells the story of His birth," Robert continued, his tone gentle, "but Carrie Grace, we can't forget the heavenly reality of who Jesus truly is. By startin' in John, we're reminded that the manger held far more than a baby. It held the Word, the very One who spoke life into existence."

Patty rubbed Carrie's back lovingly and added, "The same Word who spoke the universe into being is the One who came to dwell among us. Jesus. Emmanuel. God with us."

Robert continued, "Before anythin' existed, my precious darlin', even before a **Midge doll or Spirograph**," he shot her a look and gave her a playful wink. "The Word was already present, coexisting with God. Jesus' birth wasn't the beginnin' of His story but the revealin' of His eternal presence."

He let that sink in before finishing. "Christmas isn't just about one day. It's about a never-endin' promise. His birth was not merely an event but the fulfillment of a divine plan. The Creator stepped into His creation. To restore us…to be the Light in our darkness. And that, my loves, is truly the best gift of all."

* * *

Lydia and Carrie gathered up the torn wrapping paper, smoothing out creases as they folded each piece to save for next year. Jessie crouched nearby, salvaging ribbons and bows, stacking them neatly in a box to be reused. In no time, the living room was tidy again.

"Who wants dessert?" Patty asked, pushing herself up from her chair.

Robert's hand shot up first, earning him a raised brow from James.

"What?" Robert asked.

"I thought ya said ya wouldn't be able to eat again 'til tomorrow?" James teased, crossing his arms.

"I said *prob'ly*," Robert corrected with a smug grin. "Heavens to Betsy, who can resist yer mama's pecan pie? James, let's be honest…if ya hadn't brought that pie the first day ya came to our house, I'm not sure I would've let ya through the door."

"Daddy!" Jessie gasped, her mouth falling open before she broke into a smile. She shook her head. "Yer impossible sometimes, ya know that?"

"I do," Robert admitted with a wink. "But I'd say there was method to yer madness, havin' James show up with his mama's pecan pie."

Jessie pressed her lips together to hide a grin but said nothing.

"I do believe ya capitalized on my weakness, hmm?" he said, voice lilting with amusement. Then, shifting tones, "Now, shouldn't ya be helpin' yer mama with dessert? And make sure the coffee's dark. Ya know what Granny Williams always said…"

Jessie smirked. "I know. *Any coffee that ain't black as pitch, ain't worth drinkin'*." They finished the last part together.

"And Jessie May?" Robert called after her as she headed for the kitchen.

"Yes, Daddy?" She paused mid-step.

"I'd say that pecan pie has come full circle, wouldn't you?"

Their eyes met, sharing a look steeped in years of love and tenderness, patience and grace. A quiet understanding passed between them, bonded through countless moments of growth, and now, this one.

Because as much as Robert loved a good pecan pie, nothing was sweeter than knowing his daughter had found a love of her own.

Chapter 6
Something Old, Something New

Thursday, December 29th, 1966

Patty casually flipped through the pages of her December issue of *Good Housekeeping*, the pages barely making a sound as she turned them. She skimmed an article on Julie Andrews. Did she really want to know why this was Julie Andrews favorite time of the year? Didn't matter, she couldn't focus enough to finish the article anyway. She turned another page. A shiver ran through her, and she pulled the afghan up, tucking it around her legs. Robert hadn't lit the fireplace, so the room was drafty. She took a sip of her steaming coffee, wrapping both hands around the mug to warm them.

Try as she might to relax, her mind wouldn't stop running double-time. Ever since Christmas, the days had been consumed with last-minute wedding plans. And now, with rehearsal tomorrow, her excitement and nerves had only intensified. She took a deep breath, filling her lungs, then slowly released it.

Lying her head back against the davenport, she closed her eyes for a moment offering up a prayer of petition. *Heavenly Father, yer word says not to worry about tomorrow, for tomorrow will worry about itself. Each day has enough trouble of its own. Please help me to be still and not fret over the details*

83

of Jessie's weddin'. I want it to be perfect, but Lord, I know if this is yer will, then it already is. Please help me rest in that blessed assurance. I know that stewin' won't do us any good. I sure need to feel ya right now. As good as this all is, it's somethin' new to us, Lord, so please keep me grounded in the next couple of days. Amen.

Slapping the magazine shut and tossing it onto the coffee table, she broke the room's quiet solitude. "Remind me again, what time are we supposed to be at the church for rehearsal tomorrow?"

Jessie, who had been dozing on the davenport next to Patty, startled at the sound of the magazine and her mother's voice. "Hmm? What was that?" she asked, still groggy.

Patty repeated the question.

"Four o'clock, Mama," Jessie yawned, stretching as she sat up. "The time hasn't changed since the last time ya asked me…before I fell asleep," she teased.

Patty sighed, giving her daughter's leg a gentle pat. "I know, I just don't want us to be late."

"Mama, ya know Daddy always follows Lombardi time. We'll be there at least 15 minutes early."

Patty smiled. "I'm just so excited for this day, child."

"Me too, Mama," Jessie agreed. Suddenly, she clapped her hands together. "In two days, I'm goin' to be Mrs. Patterson," she squealed.

"Come here, my darlin'," Patty said, patting the cushion beside her. "Come tuck under my wing for a spell. I want to hold onto my little bird for just a bit longer."

Jessie grew quiet, snuggling against her mother as Patty ran her fingers gently through her hair. A subtle tingling spread across her scalp, melting into a soothing calm. Her heart still raced with anticipation, but in her mother's embrace, her body surrendered to stillness.

In just two days, she would become Mrs. James Patterson. And no matter how much life changed, she would always be a daughter, deeply loved by her parents.

* * *

Friday, December 30th, 1966, Rehearsal Day

Rita and her daughter Elizabeth knocked on the door at eleven o'clock the next morning.

The door creaked slightly as it opened, revealing Robert standing in the entryway, a warm smile on his face. "Come on in," he greeted, stepping aside for them to enter.

"Good mornin', Robert!" Rita's voice was bright with cheer. "Y'all ready for this?"

"Patty's had us up since six o'clock this mornin'," Robert chuckled, pushing the door shut behind them.

"That's about the time I got the coffee pot goin' at our house," Rita remarked, kicking off her Mary Janes and sliding them neatly on the rug off to the side. "I've been drivin' John crazy. He told me I was actin' as wild as a June bug on a string."

"Well, y'all be in good company with my wife 'cause she's been fidgety as a June bug herself."

"Forgive me for not stoppin' to chat, sir, but we have important things to do," Elizabeth cut in, patting the small bag clutched tightly at her side.

"The gals are all upstairs. Go on up," he chuckled, tilting his head toward the staircase.

"Thank you, Mr. Clark," Elizabeth replied quickly. Without missing a beat, she turned and bounded up the stairs, taking them two at a time, leaving Robert and Rita standing in her wake.

"To be so nimble," Rita said, shaking her head.

Robert chuckled. "Ya know what my Pawpaw Joe always used to say?"

Rita raised her eyebrows. "What's that?"

"Youth…it's wasted on the young."

They shared a laugh, and then Rita turned toward the staircase, opting for a more measured approach than her daughter.

* * *

Elizabeth heard giggling on the other side of Jessie's bedroom door. She knocked hastily, eager to be let in.

The door flew open and Jessie pulled Elizabeth into a hug, then held her at arm's length, beaming. "Eeeeeeeeee!" she shrieked. "Get in here. The countdown has officially begun!"

Elizabeth was tugged into the room. Patty, Lydia, and Carrie were already crammed inside. Lydia sat cross-legged on Jessie's bed, Carrie on the floor, and Patty in the desk chair. Jessie plopped down beside Lydia and patted the spot on her other side, beckoning Elizabeth to join her.

"Mama said I owe my thanks to you for organizin' this whole somethin' old, somethin' new thing. Admittedly, it's all I've thought about since Christmas."

"We've actually been plannin' this since Thanksgivin'," Elizabeth smiled, a smug look clearly revealing her satisfaction in the moment.

"I even knew about it," Carrie added proudly. "And, I kept it a secret!" She lifted her chin high.

"That is somethin', Carrie Grace!" Jessie laughed, then turned back to Elizabeth. "Where's yer mama?"

As if on cue, a knock at the door sent Jessie catapulting off the bed. She swung it open and embraced her soon-to-be mother-in-law with the same enthusiastic hug Elizabeth had received.

"Here, you take my chair," Patty offered, quickly standing up. "I'll snuggle with Carrie Grace on the floor."

"Patty, don't give up yer seat. I can sit on the floor just as easy."

"No, no," Patty insisted, shaking her head. "It's a bit cramped in here, but it felt right to gather in the room of her youth." She moved to stand beside Jessie. "If these ol' walls could talk, they'd tell of ya growin' up from a child to a woman." She cupped her hands tenderly alongside Jessie's face. "It's the perfect place for somethin' old, somethin' new."

Rita blew her nose. "Mercy, I swore I wouldn't cry today."

"Well, join the club. I swear, I've been cryin' every day since prob'ly Thanksgivin'!" Patty wiped a tear and laughed in spite of herself.

"Okay, okay," Elizabeth broke in, clapping her hands. "Enough of this sappy stuff. I'm dyin' to give Jessie her gifts. Patty, you start. Yer 'somethin' old'."

"Heavens, I'm not sure how I should take that," Patty teased with a smirk.

"Goodness gracious, that didn't come out right," Elizabeth stammered, her cheeks turning three shades of red. "Somethin' old, somethin' new…" She cleared her throat. "I just meant that you have the somethin' old…so you go first."

"Oh, I knew what ya meant." Patty winked.

She picked up a folded dishcloth from Jessie's desk and unwrapped it with care, revealing a small, faded black jewelry box. "Somethin' old," she announced, shooting Elizabeth a comical look before handing the box to Jessie. "It was my mother's, yer Grandma Williams'."

Jessie took the box with both hands, studying it reverently before lifting the lid. Inside lay a silver vermeil flower brooch, its delicate petals adorned with three ruby-red teardrop rhinestones. A swirl of leaves and a bow framed the center, where a single faux pearl was nestled among the stems. She brought her fingers up and gently traced its details.

"It's beautiful, Mama," she whispered, overcome.

Elizabeth, never one to let silence linger, stepped forward with the bag she'd been holding. Jessie carefully set the brooch on her desk before accepting the bag. She immediately recognized it from Fancy's Mercantile. The sturdy, flat-bottomed paper sack was light brown with *FM* printed in bold, navy-blue lettering across the front. Beneath the monogram, in smaller script, were the words *Quality Goods Since 1949.*

Jessie gave Elizabeth a curious look.

"Just open it," Elizabeth ordered impatiently.

The bag was folded neatly and tied with twine. Untying the knot methodically, she smoothed the top open. Inside was a neatly bundled package of tissue paper. Letting propriety slip away, she tore into it.

Responding with approval, Elizabeth clapped. "Well done!"

Jessie pulled out a pair of soft wrist-length white cotton gloves. She gasped. "Elizabeth, ya shouldn't have!"

"Yes, I should. And I did." She pulled Jessie into a hug. "Since we don't have kids, and David has a new job…well, I've gotta spoil somebody!" She winked at Jessie. "So, there! Somethin' new."

The affectionate look they shared lasted for only a moment before Lydia interrupted. "My turn," she said, her voice suddenly cutting through the quiet, drawing every eye her way. She had remained silent up to that point, and the unexpected sound of her voice jolted the room's attention.

Lydia reached beneath the pillow.

"Land sakes, you've had somethin' under my pillow this whole time?" Jessie asked, her face lit with surprise.

"Maybe." Lydia's response was sly, a glint of mischief in her eyes as she pulled out a small hair comb accented with mother-of-pearl. "Somethin' borrowed," she said softly. "I got it from Mary for my birthday. I haven't even worn it yet, but I want you to wear it tomorrow."

"I can't," Jessie objected. "What if Mary sees it?"

"I already told her yer wearin' it for yer weddin', and she was plumb tickled. So, if ya don't, she might be offended," Lydia replied, grinning impishly, looking more like their daddy than she ever had.

Jessie smiled, then nodded, her eyes shining.

"I guess it's my turn now," Rita said, stepping forward. "Somethin' blue."

She held up a delicate white linen handkerchief, its edges trimmed in ornate, handmade powder-blue tatting. In one corner, Jessie spotted the initials *JMP* stitched in elegant monogram. Her brows furrowed. Then realization dawned.

Her *new* initials.

Rita saw tears brimming and reached up, gently brushing Jessie's cheek. "Tuck it in yer sleeve tomorrow, darlin', and use it for the happy tears I know'll keep comin'."

"Oh, Rita, it's beautiful," Jessie sniffled, trying hard to hold back her tears. "I'll treasure it always." She wrapped Rita in a hug.

Stepping back, Jessie paused to take in the scene around her. The soft glow of the lamplight and the comfort and love tucked into every corner of her childhood bedroom wrapped around her like a familiar quilt. Her eyes drifted from Rita to her mama, then to Elizabeth, Lydia, and finally Carrie whose big brown eyes shimmered with unshed tears.

"Oh, Peanut," Jessie murmured, reaching down to stroke her cheek. "Now yer gettin' emotional too?"

Carrie sniffled. "No, you've been standing on my foot since ya stepped back."

Silence.

Then, an eruption of laughter, pure and unrestrained.

Something old, something new.

Something borrowed, something blue.

And with Carrie, always something true.

* * *

"I thought the rehearsal went well," James noted, grabbing Jessie's hand as he walked her home.

"I did too," she agreed, though the corners of her mouth soon dipped into a puzzled frown.

James caught the shift in her expression. "What? Not gettin' cold feet, are ya?" he teased, his eyes dancing.

Jessie shook her head. "I swear Lydia and Nathaniel were flirtin' at the rehearsal."

James stopped in his tracks and dropped her hand, his face lighting up. "Ya noticed that too!" he burst out, throwing a few excited punches in the air.

"Stop that!" she laughed. "You weren't supposed to agree with me."

"Well," James smirked, "she is turnin' into a beautiful young lady, just a younger version of you. And let's face it..." He hesitated a beat. "Nate's always kinda had a crush on ya, so it makes sense."

"James!"

"It's true," he said matter-of-factly, jerking his head to toss his hair out of his eyes. "He's been soft on ya since we was young."

Jessie's laughter faded as somberness crept into her features. She remembered how hard it was

91

when James was in Vietnam, how tempting it had been to lean on Nathaniel when she missed James so desperately. She silently thanked the Lord for giving her the strength to remain faithful.

James watched her carefully as they walked. "You okay?" he asked, wrapping an arm around her.

She exhaled softly. "I am now."

James stopped and turned her toward him. They stood facing each other, the night quiet and still around them. Jessie blinked slowly, her soft hazel eyes locking onto his. He reached up, cupping her face in both his hands. She shivered as he leaned in, their breath mingling in the cool air. He could hear the heaviness of her breathing, partly from the cold, partly from their closeness.

When his lips met hers, he tasted the sweet hint of strawberry lip gloss and she smelled faintly of rose petals. He opened his eyes and pulled back slightly, watching as her eyes fluttered open. In that moment, she was perfect beauty. And soon, she would be his.

Chapter 7
Love Never Fails

Saturday, December 31st, 1966, the Wedding Day

Robert stood patiently, waiting for Patty to come out from their bedroom. They were planning to go up to Jessie's room together. He heard the click of her heels before he saw her, and when she rounded the corner, his breath caught.

"Well now, yer just as lovely as the day I married ya."

Patty scoffed, adjusting her dress around her figure. "I believe *a few* things have changed."

Robert ignored her protest. "I feel bad for Jessie now."

Patty arched her eyebrow. "What do ya mean?"

"Well, the mother-of-the-bride ain't s'posed to outshine the bride," Robert smacked his lips. "But, mmm, mmm, mmm, she's got herself some competition."

"Oh, stop that," Patty sputtered, waving off his compliment as he pulled her close.

"Robert!" she scolded, wriggling free from his grip. She smoothed the front of her dress and tried to look stern. "You'll wrinkle me."

But she knew her expression had already given her away.

"Alright," Robert conceded with a sigh, grinning. "But later, yer mine."

* * *

Robert and Patty quietly approached Jessie's bedroom door, pausing when they heard laughter from inside. As Patty reached to knock, Robert gently took her hand. With his free hand, he rested it above Jessie's doorframe, just as he always had, and bowed his head.

"Heavenly Father, we've prayed for this day for a long time. So many times, I have asked ya to lead Jessie May to the man you desire for her. And now, as she steps into this next chapter, I ask ya to bless their marriage. May they love each other with yer everlastin' love and choose each day to walk together in faith. Amen."

He gave Patty's hand a gentle squeeze, drawing her gaze upward. Meeting her eyes with a loving look, he knocked softly. "Everyone decent in there?" he called through the door.

From inside came Karen Norraine's voice, jovial as ever. "As decent as we get!" More giggles followed.

"Come on in," they heard Jessie call.

Patty turned the knob, and she and Robert stepped inside. Jessie stood between Karen Norraine and Betty Lou as they styled her hair. Lydia was crouched behind Carrie Grace, who squirmed impatiently in Jessie's desk chair while Lydia's exasperated voice urged her to hold still.

But none of that held Robert's attention. His eyes went straight to Jessie, standing radiant in the center of the room. "Ya look pretty as a peach," he said, his voice thick with emotion.

Betty Lou smiled, a sparkle in her eyes. "Just wait 'til she gets her dress on."

"But we've gotta wait 'til we're at the church," Karen Norraine added, reaching for the can of Aqua Net. "Can't risk James seein' her."

"No siree can James see her before the weddin'," Carrie chimed in, ever the expert. "It's bad luck, ya know."

Patty beamed at Jessie. "Ya look gorgeous, my darlin'. A vision to behold." Her smile lingered, warm with pride. "But as much as I'd love to stand here and admire y'all, we best be headin' to the church. We can't be movin' at a cotton pickin' pace or we'll be late for yer weddin'."

"Or worse..." Robert added, pausing for effect. "Upsettin' Arlette."

Laughter rippled through the room, just as he had intended.

"Yes, we better not get my weddin' coordinator in a tizzy," Jessie agreed, amusement dancing in her eyes. "That would not be good. Plus, we told Elizabeth we'd meet her there at four o'clock. Weddin' bells are at five."

The girls hurried to pack up the last of their makeup and belongings. Robert offered to carry down the dresses, which were hanging neatly in the closet, but asked for a moment alone with Jessie first.

As the others began filing out, Robert crossed the room to stand beside their daughter where Karen had been moments ago. He reached for her hand, and Patty stepped forward and took the other.

95

"My sweet girl," Robert began, his rough, calloused thumb softly stroking her hand. "Today, you and James feel many things. Yer love is fresh, new, and full of excitement. But I want to tell ya something important. This feelin' won't always be the same. It'll change. A feelin' loses its luster. Over time, the shine of today will fade. There will be hard days."

He paused, meeting her eyes.

"When Pastor Mark asks if ya take each other in good times and bad…remember, always choose to love. No matter what. Love never fails. It covers over a multitude of sins. Cherish each other, forgive readily, and hold tight to trust and respect. A strong marriage isn't just about a *feelin'* of love, but a *choice*. Choose to love each other daily through thick and thin. Marriage needs to be built on grace, patience and a willingness to compromise. And, never take yer love for granted."

Reaching up, Robert gently brushed the back of his knuckles across Jessie's cheek. A single tear slipped down her face and landed on his hand. She quickly reached into her sleeve for the delicate handkerchief Rita had given her and dabbed at the tear.

"Thank ya, Daddy," she whispered, her eyes full of love. Glancing between both her parents, she squeezed their hands. "If my marriage can be even a glimpse of yours, I'll be blessed. Thank ya for bein' such a beautiful example of what unconditional love should look like. I love ya both so much."

She leaned in, and both her parents wrapped her in a tender embrace.

As Robert held his little girl close, he reminded himself that he wasn't losing a daughter today. He was gaining a son.

* * *

They arrived at First Baptist just after four o'clock only to discover it was too late.

Arlette was already in a full-blown tizzy.

No stopping that freight train, Robert thought, a flicker of amusement playing on his face as he watched her frantically usher the girls downstairs to the changing room.

The small church was beginning to fill with guests. The scent of lit candles drifted through the air, blending with fresh pine and the faint sweetness of cloves and cinnamon. Arlette had tucked satchels of holiday potpourri discreetly near the pews, letting their fragrance settle into the space. The altar was a vision of Christmas splendor with rows of bright red poinsettias flanked on either side. Garlands of evergreen were draped along the banister railings, woven with crimson ribbon and spray-painted golden pinecones. A large wreath, adorned with a burgundy bow, hung above the cross at the front, anchoring the entire scene in reverent beauty.

From the organ loft, Mrs. Penderlyn's confident rendition of "Ode to Joy" echoed through the sanctuary. The deep resonant notes filled the church with festive grandeur. Robert listened and took it all it, briefly wondering how in the world she managed to reach the foot pedals with her short little legs. The thought made him chuckle under his breath. Shaking his head, he reminded himself he probably shouldn't get caught standing around grinning like a fool. Especially not with Arlette on the loose.

He needed to go find James. There was something he wanted to say, something important, before the ceremony began.

* * *

Robert found James in the side room adjacent to the sanctuary, surrounded by his groomsmen Bobby Ray, Nathaniel, Ricky James, and David. Their voices and easy banter filled the small space, the mood light and relaxed. When Robert stepped inside, the attention shifted to him.

"It's a good day for a weddin', boys!" he declared, clapping Bobby Ray on the back. "And I gotta say, y'all clean up well, especially you, Bobby Ray."

"We were worried about that. It was a stretch," RJ quipped, landing his own slap on Bobby Ray's back.

A brief friendly scuffle broke out among them. Robert let the moment play out before clearing his throat. "Alright, if y'all don't mind, I need a word with James."

"Uh oh! James already in trouble with his father-in-law?" Bobby Ray teased, grinning.

Before anyone could answer, David corralled the others out of the room, shutting the door behind them just as Bobby Ray tried to sneak in one last remark.

The laughter faded with the click of the latch. Silence settled in its place. The atmosphere changed.

Robert drew in a breath and looked James in the eyes, his expression serious. "There is one thing I want to say to you before ya marry my daughter."

James swallowed the lump in his throat and straightened. "Yes, sir?" The humor from moments ago now respectfully set aside.

"Don't put her first."

James blinked, caught off guard. Of all the things Robert could've said, this wasn't at all what he expected. "With all due respect, sir, I don't understand. Ya don't want me to put yer daughter first?"

"No," Robert answered without hesitation. He placed both hands firmly on James's shoulders. "Son, I want ya to put the Lord first. When ya do that, yer marriage will be built on solid ground. And if yer marriage has the Lord first, it will not fail."

* * *

The church was packed, the air warm and slightly stuffy, making it feel more like a July wedding than one on New Year's Eve. Overhead, the ceiling fans Arlette had turned on rotated at a slow, methodical pace. The final trickle of guests were being ushered to the back pews amidst the buzz of seated friends and family.

Jessie's Godparents, Uncle Larry and Aunt Clara, carried the last of the wedding gifts downstairs as the church bells rang out. The echoing chimes rose above the organ music, announcing that it was five o'clock.

The side door of the vestry opened, and Pastor Mark entered, followed closely by James. All heads turned to the front, guests shifting in their seats for a better view. Dressed in his black suit, James took his place before the altar, standing tall and eager. His anticipation was growing with each passing second.

From the organ loft, Mrs. Penderlyn began playing the song they had chosen for their attendants' procession. A small smile tugged at James's lips. Jessie had wanted the song, and she was right. "Jesu, Joy of Man's Desiring" was the perfect choice for a wedding this time of year. Taking the musical cue, the wedding party began their procession from the basement doorway. James knew Arlette would be leading Jessie around back so that she could enter through the main doors.

Karen Norraine and Bobby Ray were the first to step into the aisle. As they made their way toward the front, James caught their eyes and gave them a warm nod. His stomach dipped. This was really happening. In just moments, he would finally marry Jessie May Clark. His heart raced, and though his smile trembled, it wasn't from nerves. It was from the profound weight of everything this day meant.

God truly had blessed him.

He closed his eyes for a brief moment and offered up a quiet prayer. *"Thank you, Lord, for Jessie. Thank you for bringin' us to this day."*

When he opened his eyes, Betty Lou and Ricky James were already approaching the altar. They paused briefly, bowing their heads just as Pastor Mark had instructed during rehearsal, then took their places.

Elizabeth, the Matron of Honor, appeared at the back of the church. And for a second, James hardly recognized her. The deep burgundy color of

100

her dress seemed to command the room's attention, and her hair was swept into a graceful updo, making her appear more mature than he was used to. He smirked to himself, the way only a younger brother could. He knew better. Their eyes met, and he gave her a little wink, a shared look of sentiment understood between the siblings.

Elizabeth slipped her arm through David's, shifting her bouquet of ivory ranunculus in her other hand. A few sprigs of Maidenhair fern peeked through, their wispy green fronds adding a vivid contrast to the flowers. The bouquet was bound with an ivory satin ribbon, its ends trailing softly, lending a touch of elegance against the deep hue of her gown.

She returned her brother's wink before stepping forward in rhythm with the music. With each step, she carried a quiet sense of calm, setting the tone for the rest of the ceremony. As she neared the front, Elizabeth caught sight of her Granny Fran and gave her a tender nod before she and David took their places.

Next came Lydia, the Maid of Honor.

Nathaniel, the Best Man, offered his arm with the poise of a gentlemen. Lydia's gown matched Elizabeth's in color but had a more fitted bodice that accentuated her slender frame. Her dark, wavy curls fell softly around her face. She laced her arm through Nathaniel's and smiled at him bashfully. Holding her bouquet close to her chest, she moved with anticipation toward the altar. They paused at the front, bowed their heads, then stepped to their places.

Then came Carrie, the flower girl, tossing petals beside RJ's younger brother Tommy, the ringbearer.

James had to suppress a chuckle, recalling Tommy's reaction to his gift the night before. Tommy had received a toothbrush and blue plastic squirt gun. He didn't quite grasp the sentiment, nor the humor, but it had caused quite an uproar with Nathaniel, RJ and Bobby.

The squirt gun had been brought back from Vietnam. It was the very one James had to surrender to Mr. Bieberdorf after getting caught squirting students in the hallway. As punishment, he'd spent the afternoon scrubbing the gymnasium floor after school with a toothbrush. Of course, he hadn't been the only hooligan that day with a squirt gun, but his buddies had gotten off scot-free.

Later, when James was serving in Vietnam, Jessie had somehow managed to get it back and sent it to him in a care package. His entire squad had laughed when he opened it, Jim Beau especially. James could still hear that infectious laugh.

A sudden heaviness tugged at his chest as a somber ache settled beneath his joy. Jim should have been here today. But James refused to let grief steal this moment. He forced himself to focus on all he was gaining, rather than what he had lost.

Carrie brought him back to the present with a cheerful flourish from the aisle. Her bright, youthful smile sent a surge of joy through him, the kind of energy he needed. Reaching into her basket, she scattered a bold blush of red camellia petals across the white runner and polished wooden floor. Tommy tugged on her arm to move her along, prompting a chorus of laughter from the crowd.

They made their way up the aisle, Carrie proudly emptying the last of her basket. At the front, she exchanged her basket for a small bouquet of magnolia blossoms handed to her by Patty. She turned to Lydia, flashing a triumphant grin that all but shouted she had gotten to be a *Magnolia girl* after all!

Lydia simply shook her head, a genuine smile tugging at her lips.

The music changed. Mrs. Penderlyn loudly piped the "Bridal Chorus" on the organ. A ripple swept through the congregation as guests rose to their feet, the wooden pews creaking in unison. Arlette stepped into view, placing her hands on the heavy mahogany doors. With a firm tug, she pulled them open, allowing golden light to pour in from the setting sun. And there, bathed in its glow, stood the radiant bride.

The crowd fell silent.

Robert leaned down with a smile. "I don't believe they're all lookin' at me, darlin'."

Jessie swallowed the lump in her throat, her heart pounding in her chest. Arlette gave her veil a final adjustment, smoothing the folds with a delicate flick of her hands. The boisterous strains of the wedding march echoed through the sanctuary as Jessie stepped forward.

She wore a high-waisted gown of white velvet; its neckline framed with satin ruffles. On her hands were the petite white gloves from Elizabeth, and in her arms, a bouquet of red ranunculus that stood out boldly against the white. Her veil, an exquisite veil of English illusion, cascaded from a petal-shaped cap embellished with tiny seed pearls. She was a vision of beauty and elegance.

103

James stood at the altar, captivated. In that moment, no one else existed. Behind the soft veil, Jessie's hazel eyes met his, her serene smile glowing with a quiet grace.

Robert held out his arm to his little girl. As she slipped her hand through the crook of his arm, she looked up at him with eyes full of a daughter's adoration. Lifting his chin, Robert began walking her down the aisle, his chest swelling with fatherly pride. At the altar, he gently lifted her veil and pressed a tender kiss to her cheek. He blinked back the tears he so rarely let others see. Then, turning to James, he met his gaze. The moment they'd all been waiting for had finally arrived.

"Who gives this woman to be married to this man?" Pastor Mark asked.

Robert cleared his throat. "Her mother and I do." He clasped James's hand in a firm handshake, then gently placed Jessie's hand in James's. With a steady breath, he stepped back to stand beside Patty, who grabbed his hand tightly, her other quietly dabbing at her eyes with a tissue.

Pastor Mark continued, "Dearly beloved, we are gathered here today to witness and celebrate the union of Jessie May Clark and James Theodore Patterson in holy matrimony. Marriage is a sacred covenant, a promise made between two souls who choose to walk this life together in love and faith. If anyone has any objections, speak now or forever hold yer peace."

He paused, glancing at the congregation, then went on. "Today, in the presence of God, family and friends, they vow to honor, cherish, and stand by one another through all of life's joys and trials."

Jessie's couldn't help but think back to the day James had volunteered for the army. They had already faced their share of hardships, and she wasn't naïve enough to believe there wouldn't be more ahead. But with the Lord, all things were possible. Whatever life might bring, she was ready to take this man as her husband.

"Let us pray," Pastor Mark declared. They bowed their heads. "Heavenly Father, thank you for this day and for bringin' Jessie and James together. We ask yer blessin' on their marriage, that it may be a reflection of yer love and grace, from this day forward. Amen."

"Y'all may be seated," Pastor Mark instructed with a subtle nod toward the organ.

Robert's sister Peggy, whom everyone called Peg, stood and made her way over to the organ. Mrs. Penderlyn played the opening chords of "The Wedding" by Julie Rogers, and Peg's voice soared as she sang the first verse. Jessie let go of James's hand just long enough to grab her handkerchief and dab her eyes before quickly tucking it back into her sleeve. James softly reclaimed her hands, his gentle touch grounding her.

Next came the scriptures they had carefully chosen. Jessie's Godmother, Aunt Clara, read first from the book of Matthew, chapter six, the passage on worry. This held meaningful significance to them, especially for James. While in Vietnam, Matthew 6:34 had become one of his favorite scriptures. *"Therefore do not worry about tomorrow, for tomorrow will worry about itself. Each day has enough trouble of its own."*

They wanted their marriage to be built on trust in the Lord, not weighed down by fear or uncertainty. This verse was their declaration of faith, their commitment to entrust their future to Him, no matter what came.

Her Godfather, Uncle Larry, read the second passage, 1 Corinthians 13:1-8. *"If I speak in the tongues of men or of angels, but do not have love, I am only a resounding gong or a clanging cymbal... Love is patient, love is kind. It does not envy, it does not boast, it is not proud... it is not easily angered, it keeps no record of wrongs... It always protects, always trusts, always hopes, always perseveres. Love never fails."*

Then Pastor Mark delivered a heartfelt sermon, seamlessly weaving their chosen scriptures into his message. Jessie felt the room fade as his words washed over her. It was intimate, personal, and deeply rooted in the Lord's truth.

And finally—her heart lurched. The part she'd always daydreamed of, always replayed in her mind. The moment she'd imagined a thousand times with vows spoken, rings exchanged, and promises of forever. She quickly slipped off her gloves as if shedding hesitation and handed them to Lydia. Her fingers were trembling. James took her hands in his once more and gave them a squeeze.

"James," Pastor Mark began, "do you take Jessie May, to be yer lawfully wedded wife, to have and to hold from this day forward, for better or worse, for richer or poorer, in sickness and in health, to love and to cherish, as long as you both shall live?"

"I do." James never took his eyes off her.

106

"Jessie, do you take James to be yer lawfully wedded husband, to have and to hold from this day forward, for better or worse, for richer or poorer, in sickness and in health, to love and to cherish, as long as ya both shall live?"

"I do." Jessie sniffled, unable to hold back the tears that had gathered in the weight of the moment.

As they stood there exchanging vows, James recalled the promise he'd made to Robert—to put the Lord first. With God at the forefront of their marriage, he knew one thing to be true. If God is love, then love would never fail.

Pastor Mark took their hands and joined them in his. "By the power vested in me and by the State of Alabama, I now pronounce y'all husband and wife." He turned to James with a twinkle in his eye, his smile deepening. "James, you may now kiss yer bride."

James lifted the veil that had obscured his view, revealing his beaming bride. His heart swelled as he cupped Jessie's face in his hands, drawing her close. With a tenderness that melted into passion, he pressed his lips to hers, sealing not just a kiss, but a promise.

When he finally pulled back, breathless, the realization hit him. *His wife!*

"Yeeeeee-haw!" James whooped, unable to contain his sheer elation.

Cheers and shouts of celebration erupted from the congregation. Applause echoed toward the stain glass windows. Pastor Mark's voice rang out above the joyful noise. "It is my great honor to introduce, for the very first time, Mr. and Mrs. Patterson!"

Chapter 8
Mr. and Mrs. Patterson

Patty leaned her elbows on the table, her hands loosely folded. Tilting her head toward Rita, her eyes lit up. "We did it!" A satisfied smile spread across her face as she took in the guests mingling and chatting at the reception.

The basement looked festive, with tables draped in the church's white tablecloths and accented with green and red by fresh sprigs of evergreen and cranberries. Atop each table sat a small plastic bowl in Christmas plaid brimming with Rita's buttery caramels, wrapped in wax paper by her practiced hand. Patty gave a pleased nod as she surveyed the room. "And, yer caramels are a real hit."

"Ya think so?" Rita asked, trying to sound modest, though a proud sparkle in her eyes gave her away. They were good. She knew it.

"Oh, I know so. I caught Robert's sister, Peg, sneakin' a handful into her purse, lookin' happy as a clam at high tide." Patty shook her head with a laugh. "Bless yer heart for all the time it took to make enough for every table…includin' Peg's 'take-home' supply."

"It was nothin'," Rita said with a wave of her hand. "I've been lookin' forward to this day and it made me happy to do it."

Patty's smile softened as she lowered her voice. "Rita, I just want to tell ya how thankful I am."

Thinking Patty was still talking about her caramels, Rita chuckled. "Well, darlin', if ya like 'em that much, I'm sure ya can stash a few in yer purse too." She winked.

"Oh, sorry, I didn't mean yer caramels." She shook her head. "Robert always says I change topics faster than a squirrel on Grandma William's coffee. What I meant to say is I'm so thankful for yer son. He's everythin' I ever prayed for Jessie May. You should be real proud of the man ya raised. I know Bennett would be proud too."

Rita's eyes filled with tears. "Thank you, Patty. That means a great deal to me. I'm overwhelmed with gratitude. Not only did I gain a daughter." She reached across and took Patty's hand, her voice catching. "I gained a friend too."

* * *

The reception came to an end, and guests made their way to the VFW hall for the dance. The band was warming up, playing short segments of music as they tuned their instruments. Twinkle lights hung from the suspending ceiling tiles, casting a soft golden glow over the dimly lit room. A few little girls twirled hand in hand on the dance floor, their dresses billowing as they giggled and spun.

Long tables lined the perimeter, where guests gathered with cups of punch, slices of cake, and glasses of whiskey or bourbon from the bar. The buzz of conversation, bursts of laughter, and clinking of ice in tumblers created a low, steady hum that drifted throughout the room.

As James and Jessie stepped through the doors, the bandleader approached the microphone. A sharp squeal of feedback pierced the room before he adjusted it with a quick tap. "Ladies and gentlemen, let's give a big round of applause for Mr. and Mrs. Patterson!"

A roar of cheers and clapping broke out as guests raised their cups in salute to the newlyweds. James and Jessie exchanged beaming smiles and made their way to the center of the dance floor.

The room quieted when the band began the first tender notes of "Can't Help Falling in Love." James had chosen the song not just for his love of Elvis Presley, but because he'd serenaded Jessie with it countless times during their courtship.

He pulled her close, arms snug around her waist, and they began to sway in time with the music. Everything beyond the dance floor dimmed. There was only his closeness and the gentle rhythm beneath their feet. James leaned in and whispered, "Would you like to finally be serenaded as Mrs. Patterson?"

The warmth of his breath against her ear sent a shiver of goosebumps down her back. As he began to sing softly, Jessie closed her eyes and soaked in the moment, savoring it like the sweetest thing she'd ever known. The hush that fell over the room as they danced wasn't born of formality, but of quiet reverence for the spell love had cast. Each step felt like more than just a dance. It was the beginning of a journey.

She didn't want song to end. But as the final notes faded with the whisper of his voice, James gave her a gentle hug to mark the close of the moment.

Right on cue, the band eased into "Daddy's Little Girl" by Steve Conway. Robert stepped forward, extending his large hand, and he led her into a tender father-daughter dance. Emotion hung in the room, and more than a few women dabbed at their eyes.

When the music ended, it was as if someone flipped a switch. The mood shifted in an instant. With an explosion of hoots and hollers, the bridal party spilled onto the dance floor just as the band struck up the perfect tune, "In the Mood" by Glenn Miller. Clyde, the hall manager, glided between couples, sprinkling powdered dance wax across the floor for smoother dancing. Energy surged through the room as skirts twirled and polished shoes slid across the floor, propelling the celebration into full swing.

Nathaniel spun Lydia effortlessly, momentarily forgetting the crowd around them. He couldn't take his eyes off her, how stunning she looked in her burgundy gown, the sheer fabric catching the light with every move. Her dark waves framed her face perfectly, accentuating the brilliance of her glowing smile.

And there was something more, something unexpected. The way her hips moved with the beat sent a jolt of heat through his body. The way her eyes darted toward him, then away, like she wasn't sure she should be looking, only made him want to watch her longer.

They laughed breathlessly as the dance spun to a dizzying finish, ending in a light embrace. She smelled incredible, a light, floral sweetness that clung to her skin. Beneath his hand, she was all velvet and heat. He inhaled sharply, willing himself to keep his composure.

Lydia, still catching her breath, suddenly became acutely aware of how close they were. Her heart pounded. *Surely from the exertion of dancing* she told herself. She shook her head slightly, trying to gather her thoughts.

Nathaniel stepped back, the corners of his mouth lifting. "If I may say so, Miss Lydia, ya look beautiful tonight."

Her breath caught for just a beat. "Thank you," she whispered, a warmth crept up her neck and cheeks.

Nathaniel noticed her blushing, and his pulse quickened in response. "Would ya save me a few more dances tonight?"

She lifted her brown eyes to him bashfully and offered a smile that lingered a moment too long. "I'll think about it," she said, a teasing lilt in her voice.

As she turned and disappeared into the crowd, Nathaniel stood still, watching her go. He let out a quiet breath and smiled to himself.

The night was far from over.

* * *

Jessie was out of breath when they stepped off the dance floor, her cheeks flushed with excitement. "Land sakes, that was fun."

James chuckled, running a hand through his damp hair. "Shall I fetch us some punch? I'm parched as a desert." He had barely turned toward the refreshment table when Pawpaw and Granny Patterson appeared behind him.

"James," Granny Patterson said, holding out her arms. He stepped into her open arms. "We are so proud of you. Yer daddy would be too." She pulled back, her eyes glistening, then turned to Jessie with outstretched arms. Jessie leaned in, feeling the same outpouring of love James had just received. "We wanted to say goodbye before headin' back to Ashville," Granny continued. "Ya know yer pawpaw. He don't like to be away from home too long."

Pawpaw Patterson stepped forward, his weathered hand lifting a small object. A single key dangled from his fingers.

In the dim light, James stared at it. "Pawpaw?"

"This, my dear boy, is the key to happiness…'less ya forget to pay the property taxes."

"Joe!" Granny Patterson swatted at her husband in amusement.

James let out a confused chuckle. "Pawpaw, I don't understand."

"This is the key to our family cabin," Pawpaw explained. "Been in our family for generations."

"Yer daddy loved that place when he was a boy. He took you and Lizzie there when you was youngins," Granny added, her voice tinged with nostalgia.

James frowned slightly. "I don't really remember it."

"Well, ya were mighty little the last time ya went. When yer daddy got sick, I reckon it just got to be too much."

Her voice faltered, heavy with emotion. James pulled her into another hug. "I know, Granny. I know. It's still tough." He rubbed her back gently.

Pawpaw cleared his throat, his own emotions threatening to break through. "For yer weddin' gift, we're passin' the cabin down to you and yer family." He glanced at Jessie, his eyes twinkling. Then, with a grin, he added, "This here key will open the cabin door. But James…" His lips puckered with a little smirk and his eyes danced mischievously. "If ya ever figure out the key to understandin' women, ya be sure to let me know."

Granny swatted him again. "Joseph Earl Patterson, it's gonna be a long ride home if ya keep that up," Granny chided, but her laughter gave her away. Then her expression sobered. "I know we ain't been back near as much as we should've. I'm sorry for that."

"Granny, it's okay," James said gently.

She took a deep breath, her gaze softening as she studied him. "Ya look so much like yer daddy." She choked back a sniffle. "We're just so happy we could be here for yer special day." She reached out and clasped both James and Jessie's hands. "Now, before I go turnin' this joyous occasion into a weepy mess, let's just end on this." She gave their hands a tender squeeze. "Congratulations, Grandson. We're mighty proud of ya. And we hope the cabin brings ya as much joy as it has for our family. Yer pawpaw swears it's the best fishin' spot in the county."

Pawpaw Williams cleared his throat. "Yep. It's where I caught yer grandma." He gave a quick wink and nudged her gently. "Clara Sue, we best be gettin' on. The sun don't wait for the turtle to climb up on the log." He gave James a firm pat on the shoulder. Then, his voice turned earnest. "All jokin' aside, James. Remember this—if ya ever feel lost, find the cabin."

* * *

In the quiet of their room, darkness wrapped around them. The only light was from a narrow sliver sneaking through their bedroom blinds, cast by the corner streetlamp outside. James and Jessie lay together, neither saying a word. A quiet intimacy lingered between them, the kind that came from the sacred union of husband and wife. James slid his arm around Jessie, his fingers lazily stroking her hair. His senses were heightened, yet the exhaustion of the day began to settle over him.

"That was amazin'," Jessie murmured, her breath still uneven.

James let out a sleepy chuckle. "Way better than a cold soda."

She giggled, unable to hold on to the quiet stillness a moment longer. "I believe, Mr. Patterson, this New Year's Eve is one for the books. I'll remember *this* forever."

"Me too, Mrs. Patterson," James drawled, his voice thick with fatigue. "Happy New Year…" As his words faded, his breathing changed to a slow, steady rhythm.

Jessie smiled. "Happy New Year, James. I can't wait for our honeymoon…though I s'pose it already started, didn't it?" She giggled again.

Silence. No answer. Only the gentle sound of James's even breaths beside her, his body warm against hers.

She snuggled in closer. "James?" she whispered.

Still no answer.

Jessie slid up slightly and pressed a soft kiss to the tip of his nose. A tender smile graced her lips. "Happy New Year, my love. Happy new life," she whispered, resting her head on his chest. As she replayed the details of the day, a quiet prayer filled her mind.

*Thank you, Lord, for our perfect weddin' day...*Jessie's eyes fluttered closed, then open again. *Thank you...for my husband...*She drew in a deep, peaceful breath. *Hmm, thank you...for...*

Her thoughts blurred. The words slipped away, unfinished. The prayer, quiet and incomplete, drifted with her into sleep.

Chapter 9
Happily Ever After

Thursday, January 5th, 1967, Nashville, Tennessee

It was the last day of their honeymoon, and James and Jessie couldn't believe how quickly it had flown by. They had left for Nashville early Monday morning after spending Sunday, New Year's Day, recuperating from the emotional whirlwind of the wedding. They'd still managed to drag themselves out of bed for church. They felt it was important to attend their first service together as husband and wife. Plus, Pastor Mark had teased them mercilessly, claiming he had one condition for agreeing to bump up their wedding and marry them on New Year's Eve—show up for church the next morning or he wouldn't bless their union. James had chuckled, telling Jessie he wasn't about to risk it.

They'd made it clear to both families that New Year's Day was only for the two of them. Just this once. It was their first holiday as a married couple, and Jessie had wanted the day to herself to pack and prepare for their trip. After the hecticness of Christmas and wedding festivities, she intended to use the quiet day to get organized before their early departure Monday morning. But despite her best efforts, James had managed to persuade her back into bed for most of New Year's Day.

But when the sun rose on Monday, its golden light stretching across the horizon full of promise for their adventure, they were somehow packed and ready to go. James was grateful that Robert had let them borrow his Plymouth Fury for the three-hour drive. The day had a bite to it, but the sky was bright and cloudless, making for a beautiful road trip through the rolling hills and small towns along the way.

Jessie had handled most of the wedding details, but the honeymoon? That was all James. With his love of music, Nashville was an easy choice. Not only did it offer a deep connection to country music, he knew Jessie would love the charm, romance, and endless entertainment the city had to offer.

And now, here they were, already at the end of the week, savoring their last night together in Nashville. On this final night, they sat across from each other in a cozy diner, enjoying coffee, conversation and slices of chess pie. James smiled, feeling pleased with himself as he watched Jessie eating her dessert, her eyes full of contented honeymoon bliss.

"See," he said, his voice husky, his gaze flirtatious. "I told ya I'd plan more than just takin' ya to bed, Mrs. Patterson."

Jessie nearly choked on her bite of pie. "James! Shhh! Someone will hear you."

He leaned in, unconcerned. "They're not listenin' to us. And trust me," he waggled his eyebrows mischievously, "*that* part of the honeymoon ain't over yet. Sure, our trip's endin', but I still have plans for you when we get back home."

Jessie's cheeks turned a deep shade of pink.

James grinned, cutting into his pie. "So, tell me, what was yer favorite part of Music City?"

"Hmmm." Jessie tapped her chin in thought. "Well, the Grand Ole Opry was incredible. Seein' Loretta Lynn? Definitely at the top of the list."

"Mmm-hmm," James agreed, his mouth too full to say more.

Jessie took a sip of coffee. "I saw a sign at our motor lodge that some new guy, Charley Pride, is debuting on Saturday night. Wouldn't that have been somethin'? I mean, ya never know, we might've witnessed a risin' star."

"Yeah, ya never know," James said, nonchalantly nodding. "What else?" He wasn't in any rush to see the evening come to an end.

"Well," she mused, drumming her fingers against her mug. "All the live music and nightlife was certainly entertainin'."

James smirked. "Yes, the *nightlife* was...entertainin'." His tone left no doubt about what he meant.

Jessie set her fork down, hands on her hips. "James Theodore!" She said, her eyes widening. "Yes, the nightlife was...er...entertainin'...as ya put it."

James snickered.

She rolled her eyes but pressed on. "But honestly, I think one of my favorite parts was our walks through Centennial Park with all the Christmas lights. That was the most romantic part for me. I didn't want that to end." She paused, her expression softening as she drifted into the memory. "Just you and me. And yet…the world. I feel so happy, so complete, takin' on the world with you."

James studied her, his heart swelling. "So, I did alright with the honeymoon I planned?"

She smiled, shaking her head. "It was perfect, but…" she hesitated, her gaze locking onto his, so full of love. "My absolute favorite part wasn't Nashville. It was you."

* * *

Tuesday, January 10th, 1967, The Little Yellow House on Brummel Street

When James came home from work, he found Jessie reclining on the couch. They didn't own a television, and without one, the living room was quiet. But she wasn't reading a book or knitting. She was simply sitting there, staring into the stillness.

"You okay?" he asked, concern etched across his features as he walked toward her.

"Yes." She sat up a little straighter. "Just tired."

"Tough day? Harder than ya thought, goin' full days?"

Jessie shrugged. She'd just started her new schedule working full days on Tuesdays and Thursdays. "Mrs. Penderlyn was convinced I'd forgotten everythin' over the holiday break and our honeymoon." She sighed. "So, she stayed to 'reshow' me how to do everythin' properly. I swear, today I felt about as useless as a screen door on a submarine."

James leaned down and brushed a gentle kiss across her forehead. "After all these years, she's just got her way of doin' things. Prob'ly hard for her to let go of that. But trust me, Jess, she appreciates ya."

Jessie exhaled with a long sigh. "Come sit beside me." She patted the cushion next to her. "More importantly, how was yer first day? I was thinkin' about ya all day. How'd it go with my daddy?"

James sank onto the couch with a groan. "Pretty good...but talk about feelin' useless." He shook his head. "We can joke about it, but I'm tellin' ya, I truly *am* useless. It became real obvious, real fast to me and yer daddy that I don't know a hill of beans about cars. By the end of today, I reckon he was thinkin' the porch light's on, but ain't nobody home." He sighed. "Prob'ly made him wonder who this ninny was that married his daughter."

"James, stop it. He'd never think that."

James shot her a doubtful look.

Jessie held his gaze. "Yer a fast learner. Ya always have been. Ya'll catch on. And besides, you've got a very patient teacher—my daddy."

"Well, I hope yer right, 'cause he's gonna need a lot of patience. Without my daddy around, I just never grew up doin' that sorta thing. It doesn't come natural to me."

"My daddy wouldn't have asked ya to work there if he didn't think ya'd be a good fit."

"We'll see," James muttered, a little too casually.

Jessie frowned. "Do ya think yer not gonna like workin' at Chuck's?"

"I just felt real dumb today," he admitted. "Like if my brains were leather, I wouldn't have enough to saddle a June bug."

121

Jessie laughed and nudged him. "Oh, stop it." Then, with a sudden twinkle in her eyes, she batted her lashes playfully. "I have somethin' that'll cheer ya up."

James perked up. "Mmm, that sounds promisin'." His voice dipped to a husky edge as he wagged his eyebrows at her.

"Not *that*," she said, shaking her head.

James looked disappointed. Then he sniffed the air. "Well, I don't smell anythin' cookin', so I know it's not supper."

"Actually, it does have to do with supper." Jessie leaned forward, suddenly feeling more awake than she had all day. "Bobby Ray caught me on the way home. He and Janet wanna go on a double date tonight. Said he's got somethin' important to tell us, some good news, but wouldn't tell me what."

James looked intrigued. "Really? Didn't say anythin' else?"

Jessie shook her head. "Nope."

"Well, that's unusual for Bobby," James mused. "He's not exactly known for holdin' back when he's got somethin' to say."

Jessie stood and smoothed out her skirt. "He said to meet them at Buckie's at six. I told him if he didn't hear back, we'd be there."

"Yeah, that works," James said, scratching his chin. "But now ya got me thinkin'."

Jessie smirked. "Well, look at that. Ya *do* have a brain after all."

Before she could blink, James was off the couch and scooping her into his arms, one under her legs and the other around her back. He strode toward their bedroom.

"That's it," he declared. "Yer gettin' consequences for that comment. Punishment to be determined by the offended."

"James!" Jessie shrieked, her laughter ringing through the house.

With a swift nudge of his foot, he kicked the bedroom door shut behind them. He might not know much about cars, but in this department, he knew exactly what to do.

* * *

The scent of grease and grilled meat filled their nostrils as they pushed through the door of Buckie's. The place was packed, buzzing with conversation and the clatter of dishes. From the jukebox in the corner, "Daydream Believer" by The Monkees played, adding to the lively atmosphere.

As they stepped inside, Sunny was already approaching them, menus in hand. From the back booth, they spotted Bobby Ray waving them over.

"Y'all meetin' anybody or will it be just the two of ya?" Sunny asked, her Southern drawl warm and familiar.

James grinned. "I see our party in the back, but thanks, Sunny."

Jessie bit her lip to stifle a giggle, remembering the time Bobby Ray had once asked Sunny for her number *as dessert* while ordering. Shaking her head, she fought back the laughter bubbling up inside her.

As James led her toward the booth, he glanced over his shoulder. "What's so funny? I can tell somethin's tickin' yer funny bone."

"Just thinkin' about when Bobby Ray hit on Sunny."

James snorted. "And now he's actually got a girlfriend. He's lucky Janet isn't picky."

"James!" Jessie scolded, swatting his arm.

Just then, Bobby Ray's voice cut through the noise. "James!" He stood, clapping his buddy on the back. "How ya been?" Turning to Jessie, he tipped his head. "Howdy, Jessie. If ya wanna slide in the back, ya can sit across from Janet, and y'all can visit. James and I have some catchin' up to do, mainly about his *newlywed activities*." He barked out a laugh.

Jessie rolled her eyes, perfectly in sync with Janet.

As they shrugged off their coats and got settled, Sunny appeared with a tray of waters, swiftly distributing them before plucking the pencil from her pinned-up hair and pulling out her notepad. "Can I start y'all with somethin' to drink?"

"Sunny, if ya don't mind, we'll just do waters while we look at the menus. Too busy catchin' up."

"Darlin', that's plumb fine by me." She blew a stray strand of hair from her face. "Just look at this place!" She gestured around the room, waving her order pad. "It's hoppin' like a frog on a hot griddle! I swear, feels like the whole darn town showed up for supper. Lemme check on my center tables and that front booth that just got seated. Y'all take yer time." With that, she scooted off, disappearing into the sea of customers.

Bobby Ray leaned forward, propping his elbows on the table. "Well, how are the newlyweds?"

"Yeah, we're achin' to know, how Nashville was?" Janet chimed in. "Bobby Ray was green with envy when he heard y'all were goin' there."

"Hey now, Jannie, ya ain't 'spose to reveal my secrets," Bobby Ray smirked. "But yeah, I was pretty jealous. Been wantin' to see Music City for a long time. Thought about sneakin' in yer suitcase…" He paused dramatically. "But I figured three in the bed mighta been crowded."

James shot him a deadpan look. "Jess, I don't think we were gone long enough."

With a devilish grin, Bobby Ray said, "Ya mighta come back just in time. Jessie May's lookin' *tired*." He cupped his hand over his mouth, barely suppressing a laugh.

Jessie furrowed her brow before insisting, "I think it's from startin' back at work."

Bobby Ray waggled his eyebrows at James. "Nah, I don't think *work* has anythin' to do with it. Ya gotta let her get some sleep, buddy."

Janet elbowed Bobby. "Ya never hold back, do ya?"

"Speakin' of holdin' back," James slyly deflected, "isn't there somethin' ya wanted to tell us?"

Before Bobby could answer, Sunny reappeared, pencil at the ready. "Alright, what'll it be? What can I getcha?"

Bobby Ray jumped in first. "While these numbskulls are still decidin', I'll take my usual—the Bacon Beast with a side of onion rings."

"Nothin' to drink? A coke is *usually* part of yer *usual*," Sunny asked, pencil poised.

"No, ma'am. We're watchin' our pennies."

James nearly choked. "Since when do *you* save money, Bobby Ray, by not gettin' a soda? And when ya say 'we', does that mean yer speakin' for Janet?"

Janet glanced at Bobby Ray, then shrugged. "Just water for me."

Sunny cleared her throat. "Did I mention it's *busy* in here?"

James laughed. "Sorry, Sunny. For Bobby, that is."

Bobby Ray groaned.

James rattled off his order. "I'll take the Big Bama, homestyle fries, extra crispy, a side of mayo, and…" He shot Bobby a pointed look. "A bottle of cherry Coke."

Bobby ignored him.

Sunny turned to Jessie. "And, what are ya havin'?" She chewed on the end of her pencil as she waited.

Jessie glanced at the menu. "I'll take the Buckie burger with coleslaw." She paused, changing her mind. "No, actually, make that the Roll Tide burger with the coleslaw. And a strawberry shake."

James's eyebrows shot up. "A little *hungry* tonight, are ya?"

"I am." She tilted her chin up with indignation.

"I guess so." James's eyebrows raised in surprise.

Janet ordered next. "I'll take the Double Trouble Cheeseburger with waffle fries, plus a side of yer chicken gumbo soup, please."

"Well, I'll be! With these appetites, ya'd think y'all were eatin' for two," James teased.

126

Jessie giggled, but noticed the quick exchange of glances between Bobby Ray and Janet.

Sunny finished scribbling the orders. "That everythin'?" After confirming, she gathered the menus. "I'll get yer orders in right away," she said, as she bustled off.

James leaned in and rubbed his hands together almost deviously. "Now, let's get back to the *real* reason y'all invited us out tonight."

For once, Bobby Ray hesitated.

James drummed his fingers on the table. "We're waitin'."

Janet nudged Bobby. He scratched the back of his neck and then ran his hand through his hair. "Well, umm...we, uh...that is...what I mean is...Janet...well..."

Jessie's eyes narrowed. "Bobby Ray, ya *never* get tongue-tied. What is it?"

Bobby Ray sighed. "Well...Janet *is* eatin' for two."

Silence. For a second the diner seemed to freeze completely in the moment.

Then James and Jessie blurted in unison, "WHAT?!"

"Yer...?" Jessie struggled with her words, not daring to utter *the p word*.

Janet and Bobby both nodded their heads.

"Oh man, do your parents know? Or more so," James looked straight at Bobby, "do her parents know she's pregn—" He didn't even get to finish as Jessie abruptly cut him off.

"Shhh!" Jessie hushed. "We're in public! Ya can't be sayin' that out loud, James." Then, leaning forward and placing her hand to the side of her mouth, she whispered, "But *how*?"

Bobby Ray nearly spat his water across the table. "Jessie May, I don't think ya want me to answer that."

Jessie turned beet red.

And then, something quite surprising happened. Bobby Ray's usual smugness melted. He glanced at Janet, revealing a tenderness in his eyes that they'd never seen before. Janet smiled back and he reached for her hand, his grin turning unexpectedly gentle.

"Oh, and…" he paused, momentarily hesitant to take his attention away from Janet. "There's more."

"MORE?" James and Jessie shrieked again in unison.

Bobby shifted, slipping a hand into his pocket. He fished something out and passed it to Janet under the table. Their heads dipped as they fumbled with whatever it was, their hands moving in quiet coordination. Then, a moment later, they lifted their hands, each now wearing a ring on the fourth finger of the left hand.

Jessie's jaw dropped. "YOU'RE *MARRIED*?!"

"Shhhh!" James was now the one hushing her, casting a quick glance around the room.

Bobby Ray beamed. "We are!"

"WHEN?!"

"Right after Christmas, December 28th." Bobby answered, looking downright smitten.

"WHAT?"

"But that means y'all were already married before we got married?" James shook his head in disbelief. "And ya never said a word? I don't get it, Bobby Ray."

Bobby glanced affectionately at Janet. "We both agreed that we didn't want to take away from *yer* day."

Jessie clutched her heart. "Bobby Ray, that's actually really sweet."

"Shhh! Don't' go ruinin' my reputation, Jessie May!"

She rolled her eyes. "What made ya pick the 28th?"

Janet looked at Bobby. "Somethin' about it was just…special. It was a small gatherin', only our parents and families attended. We picked that Wednesday after the prayer service because Pastor Mark agreed to marry us in the church so we wouldn't have to do the justice of the peace since…well…we kind of messed up the *order* of things." She blushed slightly. "And he had one condition. We had to complete his marriage counselin' classes or he wouldn't—"

"Bless yer union!" James finished for her with a laugh. "Yeah, we know about his conditions."

Bobby grinned. "Yeah, it was that and the fact that when we told her parents, her daddy said if I didn't put a ring on his daughter's finger real soon and make her an honest woman, I wouldn't live to see 1967." He chuckled, then turned serious, wrapping an arm around Janet. "But honestly? We're happy. Really happy."

As Jessie watched them, she could see it wasn't just happiness. It was love.

Just then, Sunny arrived with a large tray, setting it on the corner of their table to balance its weight as she passed out their orders. She stopped, glancing around at the unusually quiet table. "Everythin' alright over here?" she asked, eyeing Bobby Ray's uncharacteristic silence.

Bobby Ray's ever-familiar smugness returned. "I hate to break it to ya, Sunny, but I'm taken."

Laughter erupted around the table.

And the rest of the night? It was filled with more laughter, hearty appetites, plenty of food and the satiation of happy endings.

* * *

Friday, March 31st, 1967

James asked Robert if he could leave work early.

Robert, not being one to miss small details, had noticed James stopping by the tavern frequently on his way home and figured that's where he'd be going. He had discretely asked Jessie about James's frequency at Linny's and she'd explained he was checking up on Hank. Hank hadn't been doing too well. Robert was surprised Linny would let James in so often. However, considering the arrangement they had made for the band to play there consistently, he supposed James had just become a regular, despite not yet being of age.

Robert decided not to beat around the bush and gave him a pointed look. "Meetin' Hank again?"

James faltered, briefly caught off guard. "No, um, actually…it's Jessie's and my three-month anniversary, and…" He lowered his voice, leaning in so Chuck wouldn't overhear. "She's been so tired and doesn't feel like goin' out tonight, so I wanted to surprise her by cookin' supper. That's my gift to her."

Robert chuckled, his laughter flooding him with a wave of relief. "I don't think Patty can count on one hand—ah heck, let alone one finger—the times I've cooked for her." He lowered his voice. "Let's just keep this between us, shall we?"

Both men laughed.

Robert clapped James on the back. "I like yer thoughtful idea. But how do ya plan to keep that a surprise when Jessie's home on Fridays?"

"Mrs. Penderlyn called in sick this mornin', so Jessie's workin' the whole day. I didn't know 'til this mornin' that she wouldn't be home, so that's why I'm askin' so last minute. Sorry about the short notice."

"No worries at all, but son, do ya know how to cook?"

James smirked. "I know it's been made quite obvious that my mama didn't teach me a thing about cars or how to throw a football, but she knows her way around a kitchen."

"That she does." Robert smiled, then raised a brow. "Hopefully it goes better than yer first time changin' oil."

James groaned as Robert shot him a teasing look. Not even needing to ask, he knew exactly what Robert was referring to. The first time Robert had James change the oil on a vehicle, he'd forgotten to tighten the drain plug. He had proudly stepped back, wiping his hands like he'd conquered the world only for the two of them to hear the slow *drip…drip…drip* as all the oil leaked right back out and onto the floor. At the time, Robert had shaken his head and told him he wouldn't be shy of practice since he'd be changing it *twice*.

Robert chuckled and then added, "And make sure ya add the right ingredients and not somethin' else!"

"Boy, yer on a roll." James couldn't help laughing, but knew exactly what Robert meant by that remark. Another time, when he'd been asked to top off the oil in a car, he had absentmindedly grabbed the transmission fluid instead. Robert luckily caught him mid-pour, hollering, "*Son, what in tarnation are ya doin'? That ain't oil! Ya tryin' to give me or that car a stroke?*"

James shook his head with a grin. He was grateful his father-in-law was proving to be a patient man, just as Jessie had reassured him. Lord knew he needed it. And thankfully, no matter how the supper turned out, he was also blessed with a very patient wife.

* * *

Jessie stepped into their home, immediately met by the clatter of dishes in the kitchen and the rich aroma of fried food. "James, is that—" She didn't get out another word. A sudden wave of nausea overtook her, and she bolted to the bathroom.

A little while later, she emerged, stepping cautiously into the kitchen. There stood James, wearing her pink, flowered apron and grinning, a small bouquet of daisies in his hand. The table was already set, a candle in the center, casting a warm golden hue.

"Surprise! Happy three-month anniversary!" he announced, beaming.

Jessie's heart melted. "James, I can't believe this." She pressed a hand to her chest, eyes drifting to the cast iron skillet on the stovetop. Fried chicken…so that explained the rich, greasy smell. Beside it, a kettle of green beans simmered with strips of bacon. She lifted a hand to her nose, trying to dilute the thick scent lingering in the air and then suddenly blurted, "I'm late."

James glanced at the clock. "No, yer timin' is perfect. The biscuits were just about to ding." He grabbed a pair of potholders and pulled a tin of golden buttermilk biscuits from the oven. "See? Right on time."

"No, James. I'm *late.*"

He shut the oven door. "Nothin's burned, so yer right on—"

"James!"

Something in her voice made him freeze. Quickly setting the biscuits down, he strode to her, gently taking both her hands. Only then did he really look at her. Her face was pale, almost pasty. "Jess, what's goin' on?" Concern flashed across his face.

She took a steadying breath. "The tiredness. The extreme hunger. And now…" She scrunched her nose. "Nausea."

James just stared at her, his grip tightening slightly around her hands.

"I'm pregnant."

For a moment, silence hung between them. Then, in one swift motion, James scooped her up, spinning her around as he whooped, "I'm goin' to be a daddy!"

Jessie clung to his shoulders, laughing despite herself. "James, put me down! Yer gonna make me sick!"

He stopped, but instead of lowering her right away, he threw his head back and shouted, "*A DADDY*!"

Jessie laughed, pressing a finger to his lips. "Shhh! If John's still at work, he'll hear ya."

James was still getting used to the fact that their little yellow house on the corner of Brummel and Main Street happened to sit directly behind Fleck's Insurance where his stepdad worked. Privacy was, at times, questionable.

Slowly, James set her down, still holding her close. His voice softened to almost a whisper. "Jess, ya just made me the happiest man in Cordova."

She smiled, tilting her head up. "And comin' home findin' my husband wearin' my pink apron, settin' his manhood aside to make me supper, should make me the happiest woman in Cordova." She swallowed hard, her stomach rebelling against the rich scents. "But right now? It's just makin' me sick."

James chuckled and, without hesitation, he carefully picked her up again. Carrying her into their bedroom, he nudged the door shut with his foot, a movement that had become second nature.

Very gently, he laid her down, then stretched out beside her, his dark brown eyes locking onto hers. Almost cautiously, he placed his hand over her stomach.

"James, we're gonna be parents," she whispered, looking straight into his eyes.

He swallowed hard. His voice quivered with reverence. "In all my days growin' up, I never imagined my life like this." He began moving his hand in slow, soothing circles over her belly. "But with you…"

Jessie lifted her head slightly, searching his eyes.

A tear slipped down his cheek as he leaned in, pressing a tender kiss on her lips. "With you, Jess," he murmured. He could barely speak past the lump in his throat. "This is just the beginnin' of our happily ever after."

Appendix
A Taste of Cordova Christmas

RITA'S CARAMELS

1 cup butter
1 pound (2 ¼ cup) brown sugar
A pinch of salt
1 cup light corn syrup
1 – 15 ounce can sweetened condensed milk
1 teaspoon vanilla

Over low heat, melt butter in heavy saucepan. Add sugar and salt; stir thoroughly. Then stir in corn syrup and mix well. Gradually add milk, stirring constantly. Cook over medium heat to firm ball stage (240 degrees, approximately 12 – 15 minutes of boiling after the mixture reaches a boil). Stir constantly. Remove from heat, stir in vanilla. Pour into buttered 9x9x2-inch pan. Cool and cut into squares. May wrap individually.

OLD-FASHIONED THUMB PRINT COOKIES
(Robert's favorite)

>1 package (18.25 ounces) yellow cake mix
>½ cup vegetable oil
>¼ cup water
>1 egg
>3 cups crisp rice cereal, crushed
>½ cup chopped walnuts
>Raspberry or strawberry preserves

Preheat oven to 375 degrees. Combine cake mix, oil, water and egg. Beat until well blended. Add cereal and walnuts; mix until well blended. Drop by heaping teaspoonfuls about 2 inches apart onto ungreased baking sheets. Use thumb to make indentation in each cookie. Spoon about ½ teaspoon preserves into center of each cookie. Bake 9 to 11 minutes or until golden brown. Cool cookies 1 minute on baking sheet; remove to wire rack to cool completely. Makes 3 dozen cookies.

ICED SUGAR COOKIES (*Lydia's favorite*)

Cookie Dough
¾ cup butter, softened
¼ cup granulated sugar
¼ cup packed light brown sugar
1 egg yolk
1 ¾ cups all-purpose flour
¾ teaspoon baking powder
A pinch of salt

Combine butter, granulated sugar, brown sugar and egg yolk in medium bowl. Add flour, baking powder and salt; mix well.

Cover; refrigerate until firm, about 4 hours or overnight. Makes about 2 dozen cookies depending on cookie cutter size.

When ready to bake, preheat oven to 350 degrees. Grease cookie sheet or line with parchment paper. On a floured counter, roll out the dough to a ¼ inch thickness and cut into shapes with cookie cutters. Place cookies on cookie sheet and bake for 8 to 9 minutes, until edges are beginning to brown. Transfer cookies to a wire rack to cool.

Frosting
1 ½ cups powdered sugar
1 Tablespoon milk
Food coloring (optional)

Combine powdered sugar and enough milk to make a medium-thick pourable glaze. If adding food coloring, adjust the powdered sugar to maintain the medium-thick pourable consistency.

SALLY ANN COOKIES

Cookie Dough
1 cup sugar
1 cup shortening
1 cup dark molasses
2 eggs
3 teaspoons baking soda
½ cup hot water
1 teaspoon cinnamon
1 teaspooon ginger
½ teaspoon salt
5 ½ cups flour

Mix the above ingredients, then cover and refrigerate until firm, about 4 hours or overnight.. When chilled, roll out thick (~ ¼ in.) and use Spam can to cut out. Bake 10-12 minutes at 375 degrees.

Frosting
1 box Knox gelatin
½ cup COLD water
2 cups white sugar
¾ cup water

Mix the gelatin and ½ cup COLD water and let stand. Boil the sugar and ¾ cup water to soft ball stage (235 degrees, approximately 10 minutes of boiling after the mixture reaches a boil). Once to soft ball stage, pour into gelatin mixture. Stir and let cool. Then beat until frosting turns white and does not run. Frost cookies quickly as frosting hardens.

Meet the Author

Chanda Stelter is a devoted wife of over 25 years and the proud mother of two adult children. Originally from a small town in the upper Midwest, she grew up a country girl. After years as a stay-at-home mom, she went back to school to become a teacher. Writing was never part of her original plan, but an unexpected twist in life opened a new door.

Her love of romance, coupled with her faith-driven perspective, gave birth to her unique brand of a Christian romance historical fiction. Through her writing, Chanda aims not only to entertain, but to infuse each story with messages of hope, humor, love, and faith. Her writing will resonate with readers, inviting them into a world where history and romance intertwine, always inspired by the faith that grounds her own life.

Chanda is grateful for every reader who chooses to share this journey with her.

More Guitar Ghost Series books coming in the future:

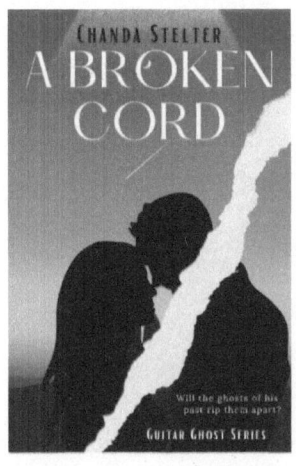

Book three   Book four

Follow and like Chanda on Facebook at:
https://www.facebook.com/GuitarGhostSeries.Chan
daStelter

Or Connect with her at:
guitarghostseries@gmail.com